GHOSTS
from the Coast

D0833157

ALSO BY NANCY ROBERTS

America's Most Haunted Places

Animal Ghost Stories

Blackbeard and Other Pirates

Blackbeard's Cat

Civil War Ghost Stories and Legends

Georgia Ghosts

Ghosts and Specters

Ghosts of the Carolinas

Ghosts of the Southern Mountains and Appalachia

The Gold Seekers

Haunted Houses

The Haunted South

North Carolina Ghosts and Legends

South Carolina Ghosts

Southern Ghosts

GHOSTS
from the Coast

· ·

NANCY ROBERTS

The University of North Carolina Press   Chapel Hill & London

© 2001 The University of North Carolina Press

All rights reserved

Designed by Richard Hendel

Set in Galliard, Castellar, and Zapfino types

by Eric M. Brooks

Manufactured in the United States of America

The paper in this book meets the guidelines for permanence
and durability of the Committee on Production Guidelines for
Book Longevity of the Council on Library Resources.

Library of Congress Cataloging-in-Publication Data

Roberts, Nancy, 1924–

Ghosts from the coast / by Nancy Roberts.

p. cm.

ISBN 0-8078-2665-0 (alk. paper)

ISBN 0-8078-4991-X (pbk.: alk. paper)

1. Ghosts—North Carolina. 2. Ghosts—South Carolina.

3. Ghosts—Georgia. I. Title.

BF1472.U6 R62   2001

133.1'0975—dc21   2001027491

05 04 03 02 01   5 4 3 2 1

CONTENTS

· ·

Preface ix

PART I. NORTH CAROLINA

The North Room
Currituck Lighthouse, Corolla   3
What Happened to Nell Cropsey?
1109 Riverside Avenue, Elizabeth City   8
A New Mystery of the Lost Colony
Roanoke Island   15
The Ghost of Station Six
Black Pelican Restaurant, Kitty Hawk   25
The Ghostly Lodger
Roanoke Island Inn, Manteo   31
Cobwebs on Your Face
Cupola House, Edenton   36
Blackbeard's House
Hammock Street, Beaufort   40
The Phantom Ship
Beaufort   47
The Ghost of Fort Macon
Morehead City   51
Where Dead Men Walk
Bellamy Mansion, Wilmington   56
The Haunted Wilmington Library
New Hanover County Public Library, Wilmington   62

PART II. SOUTH CAROLINA

Ghost of the Old Firehouse
Myrtle Beach   69

Someone Watching Over Me
Oliver's Lodge, Murrells Inlet   72

Does the Gray Man Still Walk?
Pawleys Island   78

The Legendary Hugo
McClellanville   83

The Man Who Found the Hunley
Charleston   89

The Mystery at Fort Sumter
Charleston   95

Hag-Ridden Almost to Death
Mount Pleasant   99

The Gray Host near Edisto
Ashepoo   102

A Night to Remember
John Cross Tavern, Beaufort   105

The Admiral's Wife
Anchorage House, Beaufort   110

The Hilton Head Specter
Hilton Head Island   113

PART III. GEORGIA

Olde Harbour Inn
East Factors Walk, Savannah   119

The Hanged Man at Churchill's Pub
Savannah   123

Rambunctious Ghosts
Hamilton-Turner Inn, Savannah   129

Secret of Foley House
Foley House Inn, Savannah   136

Eerie Events at River's End
River's End Restaurant and Lounge, Thunderbolt   140
The Haunted Marshall House
Savannah   143
Mystery at the Moon River
Moon River Restaurant and Brewery, Savannah   149
Sea Serpent of the Altamaha
Darien   153
The Light in the Cemetery
Christ Church, St. Simons Island   157
Bloodthirsty Abraham
St. Simons Island   161
Jekyll's Haunted Room
The Jekyll Island Club Hotel, Jekyll Island   164

PREFACE

· ·

"How did you become interested in writing ghost stories?" readers often ask. I will tell you. It all began during a visit to my mother in Maxton, North Carolina, when she told me about the supernatural experience of an old friend of hers—a Presbyterian minister.

"Did I ever mention Dr. John Allen McLean's story to you—his seeing a ghost in the old Slocumb home in Fayetteville?" she began.

"You certainly didn't," I replied, recalling Dr. McLean stopping by the house to see Mother once when I was a child. What a solemn-faced man he had been. His interest was certainly not in children but all in talking to her, so I soon escaped to go out and play. But teams of wild horses could not have dragged me away had I known this austere, bespectacled gentleman had seen a ghost!

Now some fifteen years later, Mother chose to tell me about it. It occurred during a party at a beautiful old pre–Civil War home in Fayetteville. Dr. McLean was standing alone in the center hall, or reception room as it was then called, debating a drastic career change. Should he continue his practice of law or enter the ministry? As he stood deep in thought, he glanced up and was surprised to see a beautiful young girl descending the stairs. Assuming that she was one of the guests he had not met, he watched her reach the last step and survey the room as if searching for someone.

Then, with an expression of sadness on her face, she turned and went slowly back up to the landing. There she paused and once more looked out over the room below. Then, as he stared, the edges of the girl grew dim and within seconds she had vanished. For the first time he realized he had not been watching a live young woman but an apparition!

I was writing travel features for *The Charlotte Observer* at the time, but I was so excited by this story that I made a trip to Fayetteville that very weekend to research it. I learned that the ghost Dr. McLean saw in the A. S. Slocumb house has been reported for more than a century. And it may be still appearing!

The girl on the stairs became the first of a series in *The Charlotte Observer* based on supernatural experiences North Carolinians shared with me. In the meantime, a reporter was assigned to do a profile on Carl Sandburg, who was then living near Hendersonville, North Carolina. Mr. Sandburg asked her to deliver an amazing message to me. His words were, "Tell Nancy Roberts that I like her ghost stories and I think they should be published in a book."

Mr. Sandburg's praise and encouragement have led to twenty-five books—about half of them collections of ghost stories and legends. Three regional books were followed in fast succession by seven books for Doubleday, two for Crowell-Collier, and later books for the University of South Carolina Press, John F. Blair, Globe-Pequot Press, and Narwhal Press.

Readers also ask why half of my books have been about ghosts. Because stories about ghosts, miracles, and the supernatural fascinate me. They show *intentionality* regarding the outcome of events—a loving and directing intelligence behind our own lives. This is the primary reason for hope and assurance of reward.

Despite my early journalistic skepticism about ghosts, and particularly the famous Pawleys Island, South Carolina, gray man, I later came to believe that certain families really had been warned by the gray man to leave the island before some of the worst hurricanes. I believe in battlefield apparition experiences as described in my book *Civil War Ghost Stories and Legends*. Also that the house at 507 East St. Julian Street in Savannah—which Jim Williams attempted to have exorcised and which I wrote about in *Georgia Ghosts*—really may be America's most haunted house!

Another question frequently asked is, "What are your eeriest stories?" This is a matter of personal opinion, but for me they have been "The Ghost Hand" in *South Carolina Ghosts from the Coast to the Mountains*, "The Dreaded Meeting" at the mansion built by tobacco tycoon James Buchanan Duke in Charlotte, North Carolina, and "The Ghost Lover," a story from Springfield, Massachusetts. These last two appeared in *Haunted Houses—Chilling Tales from 24 American Homes.*

But what shall I say about this new book—*Ghosts from the Coast?* Collected from three states, the stories I found eeriest to write were "Blackbeard's House," set in Beaufort, North Carolina; "The Hilton Head Specter" from Hilton Head Island, South Carolina; and "The Hanged Man at Churchill's Pub" in Savannah. The pub story is about a bare-knuckle fight. Although today illegal, these brutal events still take place secretly in remote areas of the South. Hopefully, with the watchfulness of the law, these gory spectacles may cease like the gladiator contests of ancient Rome.

Ghosts from the Coast takes place against the backdrop of the random violence of the ocean, towering waves charging toward the beach, and the steady hypnotic roar of the surf along the coast of the Carolinas and Georgia. Save for the desert, the sea, more than any force I know, shapes and bends and sometimes breaks the lives of those who live beside it. A woman recently contacted me sharing her own chilling experience at Hilton Head. (She had been amazed to read a similar story in my South Carolina book.) She wrote: "The hairs on my arms rose as I read your account." The hairs on my arms rose too as I read *her* account describing what she had seen on the beach one August night in 1997. "The Hilton Head Specter," which you will find in this book, is based on her experience.

I would like to thank the people of the coast for their encouragement and cooperation in regard to these stories and for their many wonderful letters sharing their experiences. These new stories of the Carolinas and Georgia have yielded discoveries as exciting for me as those in my first book. I never tire of writing about the supernatural and the miraculous and am grateful for this opportunity once more.

I

North Carolina

THE NORTH ROOM
Currituck Lighthouse, Corolla, North Carolina

. . . .

uilt in 1874, Currituck Beach Lighthouse has been a comfort to mariners along the dark and hazardous forty miles of coast that lie between Cape Henry to the north and Bodie Island to the south. Visible to ships from nineteen miles away at sea, the flashing light says—keep your distance. Today this once isolated area swarms with tourists, but few of them know the eerie story that took place here. It started first with one death and then another until superstition grew. This story is about the "strange feeling" people have when they enter the North Room of the keeper's house.

The families of both the keeper and the assistant keeper live in the same building, but, if this sounds a bit too cozy, it is really a duplex with each family enjoying its own private quarters. Scarcely visible from the exterior of the building, in its lovely setting of trees, is the fact that we are actually looking at two identical houses divided imperceptibly down the middle.

Historian Lloyd Childress, a tall, dignified lady, relates something that happened when she first arrived at the historic site and was showing a tour group through the house. "When we came to the north bedroom, I led the way so that they could follow and then turned and waited for them all to go in. A young man entered and then, quite suddenly, he backed out of the room! I asked, 'What's the matter?' and he said, 'Oh, I can't possibly stay in this room.'

" 'Why not?' I inquired.

" 'Because there is a presence here, and I can't be in the same room with it!' he said. He would not go in there. I went to one of the members of the board of directors and said to him, 'Do you want to tell me about any of the bedrooms in the house?'

"He smiled and immediately answered, 'Oh you must mean the north bedroom. That's where the ghost of Lovey is said to be. She was the wife of William Riley Austin, one of the last keepers stationed at Currituck. Mrs. Lockwood Powers, a friend of hers, visited her here and stayed in the North Room. Mrs. Powers, who was stricken with a mysterious illness, died during her visit, and her body was placed in a horse-drawn cart and taken home to Kitty Hawk for burial.'"

Ms. Childress continued. "A gentleman who stayed in this side of the house during the early stages of the restoration would not enter the room. It's no wonder. Did I tell you about little Sadie?" she asked, and I shook my head.

"Well, Sadie was the child of the first lighthouse family to live here, and everyone in the village knew the little girl. Her parents, George and Lucy Johnson, doted on her. Mrs. Johnson would do needlework to occupy herself, but her child was never far from her thoughts. I'm afraid Sadie was more venturesome than she should have been, and her favorite pastime was building castles in the sand not far from the surf. Day after day her mother would walk outside to check on Sadie and see her little body crouched down, small hands pressing sand together for a tower or digging a moat around an elaborate castle. Her head, with its lovely golden hair, would be bent in concentration.

"Sometimes Sadie would lose herself in the details of walls and turrets as the tide crept closer and closer. When she came home, her shoes and dress would be drenched if a sudden surge of foaming surf had caught her and with its malicious hand swept away part of her castle. The natives said she would stamp her foot in anger and shout at the sea, 'Don't do that! Do you hear me? Don't do it, I said' as she tried to replace a destroyed section of a tower or bridge.

"But one day, playing at the edge of the water, she took off her shoes to wade. There must have been a powerful riptide, for before she realized what was happening the sea swept her out far beyond her depth. Her little

No one has yet spent an entire night in the North Room of the keeper's house at the Currituck Lighthouse.

arms must have flailed out, and perhaps she shouted angrily at the water, 'Don't do that! Do you hear me? Don't do it, I said!'

"Her frantic parents searched until dusk and then were joined by volunteers with lanterns, but to no avail. It was not until the next day that Sadie's body washed ashore and was found by a local fisherman. And since the North Room had been hers, her parents laid her there before the burial.

"Several visitors believe they sense spirits in this room," continued Lloyd Childress.

So saying, she opened the door to the North Room. "At least two have received the impression of a very strong presence in here," she confided as we entered a gloomy little room with only two windows. It was as depressing and foreboding as a mausoleum in contrast to the bright world outside where parents and children chattered as they queued up, waiting to crowd into the souvenir shop or the lighthouse. There was an unreality about all that happy activity below in contrast to the gloomy aura of the room I stood in. I thought of Sadie and her bright life snuffed out by the sea. And then of the keeper's wife who died here. "Who was she?" I asked, "and of what did she die?"

"Why that is really John Wilson's story over at the Roanoke Inn," said Ms. Childress. "He inherited this lighthouse keeper's house and has been instrumental in seeing that it is restored through the efforts of Outer Banks conservationists.

"But according to the records of the keepers who were here, an unidentified keeper's wife suffered from tuberculosis, or consumption as they called it then, and finally died. There were three families stationed at Currituck at a time, and this was one of the last. The North Room also belonged to the ill young woman. I can imagine her, in her isolated quarantine, staring down at the grounds below watching others engage in all the activities for which she was now too weak. There was nothing that could be done for tuberculosis then, and people were very much afraid of it, knowing how contagious it was.

"Upon this poor lady's death every article of clothing she owned, down to her smallest possession, was thrust into a wooden barrel, which was then sealed and left in the North Room. The family moved away. Everyone had a dread of touching anything that had belonged to her, fearing that even a handkerchief or petticoat might carry the deadly infection.

"After the house was abandoned in 1938, children in the village were told, 'Don't ever touch the barrel!' Of course that only aroused their curiosity. The first thing they did was to come into this room and find the barrel. Prying up the lid, the children pulled out one piece of clothing after another— a coat, a hat, a dress, a scarf—and, wearing them, they paraded about the house. When this macabre game of 'playing dress-up' was discovered, the dead woman's clothes were boxed and burned," said Ms. Childress.

Although there have been guests here from time to time, keepers do not live in the house today; nor are they needed, since the lighthouse has been automated. Duties like cleaning lenses, trimming wicks, fueling the lamp, and winding the clockwork mechanism to rotate the beacon are now as outdated as the lighting and snuffing of city streetlights followed by the reassuring cry of "Ten bells and all is well" sung out by night watchmen a century ago.

But is all really well here at the keeper's house now?

According to John Wilson, the owner, *no guest in the house has ever been willing to spend an entire night in the North Room.*

. . . . . .

The Currituck Beach Lighthouse and Museum Shop are open daily from Easter through Thanksgiving. (During periods of high winds or thunderstorms the lighthouse tower may be closed to climbers.) For information, visit the website at www.outer banks.nc.us/curritucklight or contact the director/lighthouse keeper at 252-453-8152.

1109 Riverside Avenue, Elizabeth City, North Carolina

. . . .

Even as a stranger visiting Elizabeth City, you soon sense that a tragedy which occurred there in 1901 is alive today. Tourists stop their cars beside the Pasquotank River and stare over at the white Victorian house with its gingerbread trim. It was once the home of a young girl named Nell Cropsey. Standing on the porch you visualize her in the living room with her sweetheart, Jim Wilcox; her five sisters; and her cousin, Carrie. Nell's ghost still lingers here, a young man living in the house says. He has felt her presence on the stairs to the second floor and also in one of the bedrooms.

Tree-lined Riverside Avenue is a neighborhood that some would describe as peaceful, even idyllic. But that would not be true, for beneath its calm outward appearance the currents of the human heart, like those of the river in front of the house, once ran cruel and deep. This is the story of a girl too brash, too beautiful, and too trusting. The account is based on the court testimony of Nell's Cousin Carrie, interspersed with what Carrie's thoughts may have been as she sat on the witness stand waiting for the next question. Now, for the beginning of our story.

It was in the spring of 1898 when sixteen-year-old Nell Cropsey and her parents moved from New York to Elizabeth City. The Cropseys came from a prominent Brooklyn family and were descendants of the early Dutch settlers. William H. Cropsey, Nell's dad, chose the house that looked like a castle on Riverside perhaps because it was impressive and had a fine view of the Pasquotank River. Bill Cropsey said he had moved to the area to farm and trade.

Nell was one of six girls in the family, and, according to most people, she was the prettiest. Even before the Cropseys moved from Brooklyn she was much admired, and when she arrived, the Elizabeth City girls were impressed with how Nell kept up with the latest New York styles.

By early summer Jim Wilcox was calling on her about three times a week, and Nell, only sixteen, was probably flattered by Jim's attentions. This must have given her confidence in a new town, where she must make friends, although the son of the county sheriff was really not her equal in family background. When Sheriff Wilcox went out to investigate a crime, his son undoubtedly went along sometimes. When they arrived on the scene, they might find an accident, someone who had been blown away with a shotgun, or the victim of a drowning. It could be anything. Sheriff Wilcox had grown accustomed to seeing the ugly, brutal side of life to which the rest of us are seldom exposed. Nell's parents may not have fully approved of Jim Wilcox, but Nell was a young girl used to having her own way. After all, she didn't hesitate to go out for a walk with a boy at eleven o'clock at night.

Nell's cousin, Carrie, would remember the night of November 20, 1901, for the rest of her life. She was an intelligent girl, and now she was concentrating very hard as she gave her testimony before a packed courtroom. She had been asked to describe Nell and Jim's courtship.

"When Jim wasn't working, he would take Nell riding and sailing. The first Christmas he gave her a dish with a silver handle, and the second he gave her a gold pin with a setting of stones. On her birthday he gave her a ring on which he had her initials cut. That was the second summer Nell and the family went to Nags Head, and Jim made several excursions down to see them.

"It was on one of these evenings when he and Nell were sitting out on the porch that her sister Ollie overheard them having a quarrel. Nell said angrily, 'If you are going to act like that all the season, you can stay home!'"

Carrie had always wondered if that had not been the beginning of Nell's feelings changing toward Jim Wilcox. She did not know what he had said that night at Nags Head to anger Nell so, but later she would think that she did know, and it made her shiver.

She continued her story to the court. "I first met Jim in September of 1901, when he came to the house to call on Nell. When I came the second time, and Nell and I were walking home from town, we passed the railway. Jim saw us and came across to speak. We were talking, and suddenly I noticed Nell had turned, on seeing him, and walked way off, looking in the other direction. They didn't speak to each other at all that time. It was not until several days later that he came to the house, and then he came right often until fair time. They were very friendly at the time of the county fair.

"Then the temperance meetings at the church began. Jim was not interested in attending, but he would wait outside and walk Nell home after the meetings."

Carrie's thoughts raced on as she waited for the next question. It may have been during the meetings that Nell, for the first time, began to see Jim more clearly and decided that she wanted to break off their romance. But she probably was not experienced enough to know how to do it and not hurt his pride. It was too bad that he had overheard her making fun of him. Carrie went on with her testimony.

"One Monday afternoon Nell and I were walking home from town and Jim came toward us from the railway where he worked and walked along with us. Nell didn't speak to him, and when we got home she walked ahead into the house. Jim asked if I would go with him to the skating rink, and I told him, yes, I would go.

"On Tuesday night when he came around to take me, he rang, and the girls said, 'There's Jim,' but none of them would get up and go to the door. I said, 'Girls, I'm tired of rude manners,' so I let him in and went up to get my hat and coat. We stayed at the skating rink for about forty-five minutes, and then we went up Poindexter Street to get some fruit. On the way home, because of the way Nell had been acting toward him, I said, 'Jim, why is it Nell dislikes you so much?' He said, 'You tell me and I'll tell you.'

"I said, 'you've had a quarrel haven't you,' and he said, 'No. She doesn't like me enough to go to the door with me, and I am going to drop her.' I

What really happened on the night beautiful Nell Cropsey disappeared from this house?

said, 'You mean she will drop you,' and he said, 'That's about the size of it.' He was quiet all the way home."

There was a question from the clerk of court, and I happened to think that by repeated small humiliations Nell and even her sisters seemed to be purposely hurting Jim's pride. I guess that was one way out of it for Nell. A more experienced young man than Jim would have seen she was losing interest and stopped calling. His sarcastic remarks and retreats into silence made me wonder whether Jim Wilcox would take rejection well.

I continued my testimony. "When I got in from going ice skating with Jim, I found Nell and Ollie. Nell said, 'I certainly would enjoy a good apple,' and I said, 'Where's the fruit, Jim?' He said, 'It's in the sitting room. It's yours. Go get it.' It was passed around, but when it got to Nell, after just saying she wanted it, she said, 'No thank you.' After a while Jim went home." I thought Nell had gone from tolerating him to purposely trying to insult him.

"Just after he went out, all of us began to laugh, and I said, 'Nell, I had to laugh at you when you refused that apple because I knew you wanted one.' She was eating it when I got back from the door. I said, 'Nell you certainly ought to have seen us at the rink. We looked so funny. I am so tall and Jim is so short. I felt like an elephant going in there with that little thing.' She said, 'Why don't you just call him "squatty."' We sat and talked for quite a while before we went to bed."

For some reason Nell's description "squatty, squatty," kept going through Carrie's mind over and over.

"The next day Nell's sister Let and I drove over to town. Jim saw us and walked up when we were ready to leave. Let said, 'Why didn't you come over and harness the horse for us, Jim?' and he said, 'I have played lackey long enough.' He got up in the back of the buggy.

"Staring at me, he said, 'You are a nice girl in a very cold sort of way.'

" 'What is the matter, Jim?' I asked.

" 'Listeners never hear any good of themselves,' he said. 'As I left last night, my cigarette went out, and I stopped to light it and heard what you said.' I said, 'I'm sorry if I hurt your feelings.' Jim Wilcox had heard me call him "that little thing" and heard the girl he had dated for two years say, 'Just call him "squatty."'

"He shrugged his shoulders. 'Oh, Jimmie doesn't care,' he said.

"But I think he really did care. Any man would have.

"When we got home, he went in with us, and Nell was playing the harmonica, so I played the mandolin. Nell said, 'We will have fun on the Old Dominion boat. We will play and then pass the hat around.' We laughed. Jim suddenly left."

I think we were probably unkind to anticipate our pleasure on the trip we were going on without him. Nell seemed to enjoy remarks of this sort.

"About eight o'clock that night [November 20] he came back. Everyone gradually went out until just Jim, Ollie, Nell, and I were left in the room. I noticed how quiet he was.

"Once he was smiling, and I said, 'What are you smiling at, Jim?' He said, 'Was I smiling? I didn't know it.' Then he said something about drowning. He told us he was nearly drowned one time and what a fine sensation it was. Nell said she would never want to drown, as all her hair would come out and she would look like a fright, and she wanted to freeze to death." I thought that an odd comment for anyone her age to make.

Carrie concluded her testimony.

"I said some nonsense, and in a little while I went upstairs. I remember it was a bright moonlit night. Mine is the room over the sitting room, and the shutters were open. In about twenty minutes I went to bed."

What happened next is filled in for us by Nell's sister Ollie's testimony.

"At eleven o'clock Jim Wilcox took his hat from the rocking chair and started out. When he got in the hall, the door was partly open. He walked out and said, 'Nell, can I see you out here a minute?' "

Nell had looked at Ollie but said nothing and gone out into the hall with Jim Wilcox. She was never seen alive again. This was the first time she had gone to the door with Wilcox since November 7, although he had been at her house every other night. Ollie thought her sister had gone upstairs ahead of her. Carrie heard Ollie come up and did not wake again until she "heard a terrible confusion of voices outside." Nell was not in her bed, nor could anyone find her in the house or outside. The river was dragged, but Nell's body was not recovered. It was found several weeks later, tied to a stake, floating facedown, about fifty yards from shore almost in front of her home. Although many people thought Jim Wilcox was guilty and he was sent to prison, he steadfastly maintained his innocence for the rest of his life.

It is hard to look at this town today and picture its saloons and lawlessness in 1901. Nell Cropsey went out alone after eleven and was never seen alive again.

The son of the family now living in the Cropsey house believes that the spirit of the dead girl sometimes walks behind him up the stairs to the second floor, and he has felt her presence in his room. "It is a sad spirit," says he. "I hope that one day Nell may be freed from this house and from any memories of the night she was murdered a century ago."

"Can you tell me who killed me?" the girl who plays Nell's ghost asks in the annual October Ghost Walk drama, as she ascends the inside stairs. If the old house knows, it does not answer. Jim Wilcox was convicted, served his time in jail, and later killed himself without telling whatever he knew. Some are uncertain even today that the right man was sentenced. All anyone knows is that it would take the most callous, cruel person to strike this girl a blow on the forehead and toss her body into the Pasquotank River.

There is more than one lesson to be learned from the story of Nell Cropsey. According to a quote from the book *Into the Sound Country*, by Bland and Ann Cary Simpson (Chapel Hill: University of North Carolina Press, 1997), mothers have cautioned their daughters, in the years since the crime, to make sure their date sees them safely into their own house, *"Lest you wind up out there dead in the sound like that Nell Cropsey!"*

But somehow the words of the ghost of Nell still cry out for the answer to her tragic question.

"Can you tell me who killed me?"

. . . . . .

This house is private property and not open to the public.

. . . .

This is a story of why and how a young single woman in sixteenth-century England decided to leave her family and embark on the great adventure of her day.

As he was becoming an old man, the secretary to the lord of a great manor decided to teach a young girl named Rose Payne to read and write so that there might always be someone to take care of his lordship's accounts and write his receipts. The Payne family were good people, serfs bound to the soil who lived in a small cottage not far from the manor house. Normally it would have been Rose's brother, Rolfe, who would assist the aged secretary, but the boy was born simple. Rose was bright, and that is how a girl in the late 1500s came to be one of the few people in the England of her day who could read and write.

She wrote the daily receipts for items his lordship sold to surrounding landowners or purchased from merchants, and due to her frequent presence in the manor she met, and fell in love with, the lord's son, Philip. But she soon discovered his lordship had more ambitious plans for Philip than marriage to the daughter of a serf. Young Philip had been engaged since he was nine to a child of five, the daughter of a wealthy adjoining landowner. When his lordship saw Rose and his son together he was much disturbed. Calling Rose aside, he explained the impossibility of such a romance.

He offered her the gift of freedom for her family and, if she chose, a free passage for herself to the New World. Although she knew a deep sadness, Rose Payne wasted little time feeling bitter. She had never dared aspire to marrying Philip, even though he had led her to dream such a thing might be possible. But fortunately Rose had developed a vision. She saw herself rising above her circumstances through her newly acquired skills of reading and writing. When presented with the opportunity to cross the sea to a new land, she accepted eagerly. What did the daughter of a serf have to look forward to in England, where customs of class and family bound each person from the cradle to the grave?

"I want you to know you don't have to go on this voyage of colonization if you choose not to," said her father. "Your mother's sister would see that you got on at the Fitzgilbert manor house where she serves. Do you really want to be one of this group of colonists leaving for the New World, Daughter?"

"Aye," Rose replied firmly, and her heart leaped at the chance!

Her father drove her in the farm wagon to London to embark with the other colonists on the first stage of her journey. Arriving just before noon, she and her father walked along the street. Rose must have stared at her first view of the bustling, rough-and-tumble city of London. Fine ladies drew up their silk skirts to keep them from being dirtied by the muddy thoroughfare, smelly fishmongers and peddlers raucously shouted their wares, hard-faced men and women stopped people and begged. A ragged woman lurched into Rose and snatched at her pocketbook, but the girl managed to shake free of her. London was no place to be out in alone, she thought, and she shrank from the horrors of the plague-ridden city. Surely the New World would be a better, cleaner place for the eyes than this.

Rose Payne and the other colonists left Portsmouth, England, on April 26, 1587, and reached Roanoke Island on July 22. Sunburned to such a dark hue that she hardly recognized herself, Rose had learned something about the sea and how to help the men haul the yards forward and trim sail. She lined up with the others in front of the dunes on the beach while Ananias Dare called the roll.

"Elenor Dare, Henry Berrye, John Sampson, Margaret Lawrence, Ambrose Viccars, Elizabeth Viccars, Peter Little, Martyn Sutton, William Dutton, Rose Payne . . ." Rose Payne listened until one hundred and at least a score more had been accounted for. Among them were couples, single men, and a handful of unmarried women. "I am one of the few," Rose thought, looking at Agnes Wood and Jane Mannering, who were also sin-

The drama The Lost Colony *can give us only some of the possible answers as to what may have been the fate of the colonists who came to Roanoke Island in 1587. (Photograph by Bruce Roberts)*

gle. She had discovered on the voyage that they were brave, stalwart girls whom she could rely upon.

What a relief it was to reach land, although of the group, Governor John White, James Lasie, and probably John Wright were the only ones who had ever seen this island before. The captain of the ship, Simon Fernandes, was an unsavory character with whom Governor White continually argued. In fact White's decision to hire this man would prove a fatal error. On the voyage, White had problems restraining Fernandes from acts of piracy whenever the fellow saw a ship worth plundering. Now, rascal that he was, he left all the settlers at Roanoke Island, stubbornly refusing to carry them on to their original destination.

Fernandes had agreed to take them to Chesapeake Bay to join an already-established settlement. Leaving them at Roanoke, where there were no English settlers, and in the month of August, meant disaster. They could not plant and grow corn—which they would need as a staple crop, just as it had always been a staple for the Indians—until the following summer. When the colonists' small store of supplies was exhausted, they would be dependent on whatever the Indians could share with them. The tribe on the nearby mainland was hostile, and Manteo's community of friendly Indians on Croatoan Island was a day's sail away.

Many of the colonists grumbled that too little thought was given to practical matters when they arrived. Instead, much time was taken up in the first weeks with lengthy celebrations. There was Manteo's baptism and the christening of Virginia Dare, the first child born on the island. Then there was the ceremony of presenting the island of Roanoke to Manteo, the Indian who had become the colonists' friend and who was acting as Queen Elizabeth's trustee. Meanwhile, irreplaceable supplies were dwindling, the days of good weather were being squandered, and hurricane season was on the way. Time was running out.

White had never planned for the permanent colony to be located here. They were to settle fifty miles farther north, where they would join other colonists. There were many reports of an English settlement and fort on Chesapeake Bay. According to John White's maps, the route would be through various Indian villages and along the southern edge of Chesapeake Bay to the site of Skico'ac, a large settlement of the Chesapeake tribe. White, the explorer, knew something of the Chesapeakes' language, and many of the colonists had been taught useful Chesapeake words and phrases during the voyage from England.

Leader and governor of this new effort to establish a colony, White was by profession a talented artist and at heart an ambitious adventurer. His ambition had already been rewarded by his incorporation into Sir Walter Raleigh's company, which promised grants of five hundred acres of land—Indian land—to Governor White and his twelve assistants. In addition each assistant had been accorded the status of "gentleman," a corps of men of rank who accompanied the monarch on military expeditions or other important occasions. This honor was of more use in England than in the wilds of this new and primitive country.

Governor White's daughter, Elenor, had just married one of his assistants, Ananias Dare. It is surprising that White allowed his daughter to be part of such a dangerous venture in the first place. The presence of few women among the colonists indicates that many of the men had decided not to risk the lives of their wives and children. Despite the attractiveness of land grants to colonists coming from a country where land was primarily in the hands of the nobility, only 118 of the expected 150 people undertook the voyage.

Single women like Rose were perhaps the most determined to go and had the least to lose. All they could aspire to in England was tilling the land that belonged to the lord of the manor or life as house servants. Their modest hut or tiny cottage, its furnishings, their clothing, whatever possessions they had were provided by the owner of the estate. A few were permitted to work for wages and keep part of the money. Some finally succeeded in buying their freedom, while a few ran away.

Without even the tools and conveniences they were accustomed to in England, the girls found ways to help each other on the voyage. When they reached the abandoned settlement of the first colonists, they set about repairing the damage wind and seawater had done to the cottages of the 1585 settlers. Rose, who learned how to haul yards and trim sail when help was needed on the boat on the voyage over, had inherited her father's skill with her hands.

Agnes came from a family that tilled the soil for a manor house, and she was frustrated at not being able to sow any of the seeds she had brought from England in the short time they were to be here. She recognized edible wild plants akin to some she knew in England. Jane's father was a woodsman and trapper, and more than once she fed the others and won admiration through her ability to trap small animals.

Life on Roanoke Island, exposed to the heat, the wind, and the sea, was totally unlike anything they had expected. Those of humble birth began adjusting to the hardships more readily than those of more gentle birth, who had less experience in working with their hands.

It was evident from the first that the colony was going to run out of food, but for some weeks the problem seems to have been ignored. The only solution was for someone to go back to England and return as soon as possible with desperately needed staples, seed, tools, and other stores. Governor John White was the person best able to wangle the supplies, and finally it was decided that he would go back to England and return with what was needed. It was necessary for him to take some of the single men as his crew for the voyage back, although this left the remainder of the small group more vulnerable to Indian attack.

White probably appointed the man he considered the most trustworthy of his assistants, Ananias Dare, to lead the colonists in his absence. Ananias was his son-in-law, and White undoubtedly feared his daughter would elect to stay with her husband, despite the welfare of their infant daughter, Virginia. He was right.

According to the examination of John White's papers in later years, he knew that the colonists were preparing for a fifty-mile journey to a settlement on Chesapeake Bay. He left general directions along with a crudely drawn map. The colonists who remained must reach it or starve to death. As White hugged his daughter and granddaughter and told Ananias goodbye, he had no idea that his voyage back to England was to take six months. During the trip he encountered an accident, pirates, and bad weather, and he was blown off course. Finally he arrived in Ireland rather than England.

Ananias's leadership abilities must have been sorely tested soon after his father-in-law left. The colonists could not agree on where to go. In any case, we can imagine that some wanted to stay and await the return of Governor White with their supplies. Ananias and Elenor were possibly among them because of the presence of a new baby in their lives. Ananias may have thought it best to wait here so that his wife's father would know where to find them upon his return.

Finally, after a number of months had passed and food ran low, they doubtless began to lose faith in White's returning with food within six months. It would certainly have been tempting to sail to the tribe of Manteo and their Indian friends at Croatoan, now Hatteras Island. Having lived two years in England, Manteo would be a link between them and his tribe. The colonists would expect to be taken in as friends at Croatoan Island, where Manteo's mother was chief of a village. They would be granted food and refuge there, near what is now the town of Buxton.

And so when John White eventually returned to Roanoke in 1590, he found only some iron cannon remaining where the settlement had been.

Later a wooden chest, filled with papers and several coats of mail, was found buried beneath the sand. The colonists would normally have taken the chest with them, for the suits of mail could be melted down into bullets, although for a small boat the mail might have proved too heavy to take. We have no answer as to when they left.

There is no evidence of a sudden attack upon the colony by hostile Indians causing them to flee. If that had been the case, they would have added a cross to signal distress when they carved CROATOAN on a tree before they left. Either their departure was the result of a studied decision to join Manteo's tribe at Croatoan or they all perished in a hurricane. If they lived with the Indians, in the several years that passed until White's long-delayed return—not in six months, but almost three years later—the colonists would probably have adopted Indian ways and gradually merged into the life of the tribe.

And now we consider an entirely new story.

White's papers indicate that in this colony were a number of men and women who were planning to leave right after his departure for England. After listening to Governor White's report of a pleasant settlement beside Chesapeake Bay, some fifty miles to the north—White seemed convinced of its existence—one group of colonists decided to attempt to find it. They hoped to join other English settlers there.

Knowing Rose Payne's temperament and courage, let us assume she eagerly cast her lot with them. She had some knowledge of sailing, perhaps even in the small two-masted vessel called a pinnace that had accompanied the larger ship on their crossing from England. It could carry about thirty-five passengers. Some of the other girls may well have joined her in thinking that this was their best choice to avoid starvation or confrontation with hostile Indians. To approach the Chesapeake by water, the pinnace would sail across Albemarle Sound, enter the mouth of the Chowan River, and then proceed north toward Chesapeake Bay.

The colonists had listened to Governor White describe this plan just before he left on August 27, 1587. He had meant to try it himself. It had also seemed practical to Governor Ralph Lane, the leader of the earlier colony.

Currituck and Pamlico Sounds were too shallow to navigate and the currents of the Roanoke River too treacherous. Since the Roanoke headed west, the Chowan River was the best northern route.

It may have been mid-September when Rose packed her few possessions and prepared to leave Roanoke Island with the adventurous group she had chosen. As she parted from the colonists who had decided to wait for Governor White's return with provisions, or possibly join Manteo on Croatoan, she eyed the waters of the sound with apprehension. In recent weeks she had learned some of its moods. The wind had been rising all morning and the waves were dark and choppy. Flocks of birds flew high above her head toward the mainland. Had the birds received some secret warning of bad weather to come? Did these signs mean they should leave now on their trip or delay it? Surely there were colonists wiser than she. She would have to trust their judgment.

As Rose packed, she held up one of the few dresses she had brought from England, made of pale, sea green flax, and touched it to her face. It was the dress she had worn on her last meeting with Philip, the lord of the manor's son. She felt a twinge of sadness. Suppose he came to Virginia someday and saw her after she became a fine lady in the City of Raleigh, perhaps then . . . but she knew it as a vain hope. One of the first of perhaps thirty to board, she felt the motion of the ship under her feet. Memories of the voyage from England came back to her, and it was good to be on the water again. Finally, sails set and a strong wind at their back, she watched the pinnace round the end of the island and nose into the sound. Its usually smooth water was a dark pewter gray and rough. The trip up the Chowan River was only a day's sail, which presented far less danger from hostile Indians than a trip by land. When they reached the closest point to Chesapeake Bay, then they would leave the ship and walk the rest of the way—a journey of about three days. As they went, she and Jane would hunt, trap and fish to provide food.

Two men who stood at the rail near the girls spoke of hoping to receive aid from the Chowanokes and other friendly tribes, but one reminded the other that "Governor Lane's murder of a powerful Indian has hurt our relations with them."

By noon the next day, the wind was reaching hurricane intensity. "Hurry! Furl the sails," shouted Rose to a young Welshman near her, but even as she grasped a rope herself, she saw he was no sailor. Drenched by torrential rain, they sped through the water with frightening speed, gusts causing the sails of the pinnace to billow and strain at their ropes. The ship tossed wildly beneath them, and they were soon clinging to the rigging for their very lives. The wind rose until the boat was racing along before it.

Suddenly the terrified girl glimpsed ahead what must be Holiday Island as she remembered it from Governor White's map. From out of the storm roared a dark, swirling column of wind. With a loud whirring sound it hurled the ship aloft. Now it was airborne. Pitching, twisting, soaring, it disgorged its passengers in every direction, tossing them out like rag dolls.

If there had been an audience watching this horrifying spectacle, they might not have believed their eyes. Who could have imagined an airborne sailing vessel headed in the direction of Holiday Island? Then the fierce hold of the tornado finally loosened, allowing the ship and its contents to plummet behind a curtain of trees in the depths of that yet-unexplored and mysterious swamp called the Great Dismal.

The schooner could well have been lifted and carried some distance by one of the tornadoes that hurricanes often spawn. Pilot Don Upchurch of Ahoskie, North Carolina, cites a storm surge that during one hurricane carried a house twelve miles up the New River. He says, "Lifted with sufficient force by wind, anything can fly."

Three centuries later, in the mid-1800s, an astonishing discovery was made. The aged, rotting hulk of a two-masted pinnace was found in the Dismal Swamp not far from Acorn Hill in Gates County. Its location was reported to be ten miles from navigable water. Some fifty years after the discovery, a shoemaker and his son in Gates County stood staring in amazement at the ancient rotting spars and brass fittings. They did not know that the old brass on the ship came from vessels of 350 years before. They had no idea of the importance of their finding!

Brass nails for shoes was all the father and son were thinking about, and they stripped the ship of them. They took them back, along with other brass fittings, to Bennett Brass near a small North Carolina crossroads called Sunbury. Here the Chowan River intersects with Bennett Creek. Even today, there may be shoes, once worn on colonists' feet, lying buried in the mud. The source of Bennett Creek is Dismal Swamp; its bed is still there. Upchurch believes the pinnace the shoemaker stumbled upon belonged to the 1587 Lost Colony. Perhaps the remains of courageous Rose Payne and her sister colonists are at this very moment somewhere in the Great Dismal, the swamp shrouded in mystery.

Don Upchurch of Ahoskie has devoted years to researching the mystery vessel of the Dismal Swamp. He has done satellite imaging of the area, and the bed is shown on the computer. This is lowland, and there are still trees there. It is somewhat dried up, but Upchurch believes that at an earlier date a ship could possibly have navigated it. Ships of the pinnace type drew only about four feet of water. Roanoke Island and the site where the vessel was seen are only ninety-seven miles apart, and between them lie the Albemarle Sound and the Chowan River.

Rose Payne really was one of the colonists, although details of her previous life and her eventual fate are speculation. We do know she must have had little or no hope of anything better at home in England, for she risked her life making this voyage. If someday we learn more of this mystery, perhaps we might discover a happier ending for the brave Rose.

In a storm in 1815, which made landfall near Swansboro, North Carolina, a house was carried by a storm surge from the Onslow area nearly twelve miles up the New River until the house reached Stone's Bay. Water is pushed up rivers and sometimes goes an incredible distance inland during hurricanes. A greater ability to keep visual and statistical records of hurricane wind intensity and storm and tornado damage during the last half-century has led to estimates of wind speeds as high as 200 miles an hour. When the Labor Day Storm of 1935 washed over the Florida Keys on September 3, there was a surge of water twenty-five feet high and a death toll as high as 408 lives. In fact we don't even know the upper limits on statistics like these, according to a book by Jay Barnes, entitled *North Carolina's Hurricane History* (Chapel Hill: University of North Carolina Press, 1995).

Black Pelican Restaurant, Kitty Hawk, North Carolina

. . . .

This story is about a dark episode in the history of one of the seven lifesaving stations built along the Outer Banks. Lifesavers, although lacking professional training in the 1870s, and often the rescue equipment they badly needed, were legendary for their bravery. But they were also very human—subject to anger, jealousy, and that fierce pride the sea so often breeds in men.

Old Station Six, later transformed into a restaurant called the Black Pelican, still retains part of the early building, its photographic history—and its ghost!

In 1884 James R. Hobbs was the keeper of Station Six. He was a man accustomed to respect from his lifesaving crew, and when he gave orders he expected instant obedience. The crew's lives, and those of the shipwreck victims, were at stake each time they launched their small craft into the raging sea.

It was rare for there to be any serious disagreements, but in July of 1884 antagonism erupted between Hobbs and a young surfman named T. L. Daniels. The dislike that sturdy, broad-shouldered Hobbs and surfman Daniels felt for each other ran deep. Daniels, a tall, handsome fellow with curly brown hair, was ready enough to go out in the boats when a shoaled ship and its passengers' lives were at stake. But a roguish smile often lurked in his eyes and curled the corners of his mouth, announcing to the world that he neither needed nor wanted orders from anyone. This attitude so irritated Keeper Hobbs that it made him watch Daniels with a more critical eye than he did any of the other men.

Daniels soon noticed this, and it brought out all the little rebellious ways to which he was by nature prone. If the keeper had been a more perceptive man and Daniels less cocky, the surfman might have gained maturity under Hobbs, who was an excellent seaman. But that was not to be, and finally the dislike the two men harbored for each other loosed its moorings. Hobbs had an attractive wife of whom he was inordinately jealous, and whenever he imagined that the young surfman stared at Mrs. Hobbs overly long, the captain would retaliate by treating him harshly. Daniels noticed this weakness and began to play upon it in many subtle ways.

On one occasion someone was needed to take Mrs. Hobbs home from the scene of a shipwreck where she had been watching the rescue. As fate would have it, Daniels was the one to escort her home in a carriage. While he did so, he was chewing tobacco, and because of carelessness, or the direction of the strong wind, he accidentally spat tobacco juice upon the full skirt of Mrs. Hobbs's dress. She told her husband about it. Early the next day rescue work continued, but when it grew too dark to put out the boats, the exhausted crew all walked back to Station Six for a drink.

Here the captain angrily rebuked Daniels for the incident in the carriage.

"Your wife wouldn't need to worry about keeping her skirts clean if she handled them like a lady," was Daniels's crude retort. This insult to his wife so infuriated Keeper Hobbs that he reached for his revolver on the mantel, took aim, and, before the horrified eyes of the men, shot Daniels dead. Blood spattered everywhere—on the station floor, on the wall.

In a state of shock Mrs. Hobbs began to wipe it up with the help of some of the lifesaving crew. The surfmen discussed in hushed tones the problem of what to do with the body. The wind had abated, so they decided to row it out in one of the boats and bury it at sea. Back from their grisly task, they slept briefly and reported to the station just before dawn.

There was no outside observer and no law enforcement within miles in these early years of the lifesaving service, so the surfmen's testimony and the keeper's, together with that of his wife, cleared Captain Hobbs. But ac-

Is the ghost of a young lifesaver the cause of weird events here at the Black Pelican Restaurant?

cording to many who have owned or worked in old Station Six, the spirit of the impudent young surfman is still there.

In recent years the station has become a popular restaurant. A couple dining at the Black Pelican in June of 1999 talked with waitpersons who claim to have had their own experiences with the ghost. Two former owners have seen enough to be convinced.

When Mimi Adams of Kitty Hawk first bought the old station for a restaurant, she was well aware of the tales that have been told for years about Station Six. "Claire Sutton, who owned it when it was a bed and breakfast, said to me, 'Mimi, maybe I should tell you something about that place' and I said, 'Claire, if you are going to say there is a ghost there, I've already met him.' I was sitting at the bar and only one guy had come to work. We were trying to get the restaurant open. Suddenly all the lights, refrigerator cooling system, everything came on. 'There's got to be someone here,' my new employee said, his face white. 'There's got to be a ghost!'

"'That's got to be hogwash,' I said, and at that moment a heavy barstool near me overturned and a gust of icy air rushed past. That was my introduction to the ghost of Station Six. From then on I knew something was really there."

An attractive, energetic woman whose dark hair is tinged with chestnut, Mrs. Adams talks about her years as owner of the Black Pelican Restaurant with nostalgia. "We specialized in fine seafood dishes and a distinctive atmosphere. I decorated the old station with reproductions of early black-and-white photographs depicting the rich history of the Outer Banks."

Mrs. Adams describes the house where the station keeper and his wife once lived as a tiny place on Kitty Hawk Road over on the north side, near where the old post office used to be. "A girl who once worked for me lived in it. She told me the house was haunted and said, 'Sometimes in the small hours of the night, we would wake up to hear raised voices coming from the loft above. They always sounded like a man and woman quarreling. On and on they would go, but the words were never distinct enough to be understood.' The young woman always wondered if the keeper and his wife were arguing about his murder of Daniels.

"The old part of the restaurant is where it occurred," continued Mimi Adams. "That is where the lifesaving station once was. When I owned it, the wait staff would vacuum in there at the end of the evening. As they cleaned the carpet, their vacuums would often turn off mysteriously. The same thing would happen at the keeper's house, so I began to feel that the ghost must hate the sound of a vacuum!

"One night I entered the dining room while the cleaning was going on, and suddenly the table cloths began billowing as if lifted by a gale wind. Then our hanging plants began to swing wildly, yet not a window was open! This often occurred at closing time. On the other hand, I would sometimes arrive early in the morning at the empty building and walk into a bathroom where I had heard the toilet flush just in time to see water swirling down the commode!

"The bar was one of the ghost's favorite places. I may as well call him

Mr. Daniels—he's the only one I can imagine it being. Tammy, one of my bartenders, would have all the ashtrays cleaned, washed, and upside down at the end of the bar before she left. Several times *she saw the ashtrays right themselves and go sliding down the gleaming wood of the bar*! Tammy knew then that *he* was around. For a while we had overhead glasses hanging from a rack above the bar. The bartender once reached up and got a glass, placing it on the little rubber mat. From an upright position, the glass did a complete somersault! About ten customers saw it, and they were stunned. They were all saying things like, 'What kind of magic do you do in this place!' I wondered myself.

"One night the bar was so busy that I had two bartenders working. The space was narrow, and they had to say 'excuse me' every time they passed each other. The male bartender said to the girl, 'Just a second. I'll move out of your way.' Then he called out to her, 'Let go of my shoulder!' It was like a comic movie because she was nowhere near him. She was at the opposite end of the bar! And that's the way the ghost of Station Six behaves. He was a brazen, sassy sort of fellow anyway.

"I was always told that surfman Daniels was murdered in the old part of the station, and that does seem to be where he is most active. He was shot by Keeper Hobbs in the room at the south end of the building. The first year I owned the Black Pelican, I kept the old carpet, planning to replace it later. It had a spot that the cleaning person would wash away but that always returned. One morning I pointed out to a waitperson that a customer had spilled a decanter of red wine on the carpet beside one of her tables. 'That red stain appears fresh,' said I. She stared at me and said, 'Mimi, nobody at that table drank red wine all night!' I discovered that every time it rained the stain reappeared, and I heard later that the table had been part of the furniture in the old station."

Mimi gazed out at the ocean in front of the Black Pelican as if her thoughts were far away. "I always wanted to set the ghost free, so at one time I found someone to exorcise it. They said it had to be done on the night of the darkest moon, and the date that fell upon was to be a night the week before Christmas. I was reluctant to do it that close to a sacred holiday and soon began to have misgivings about having it done at all." Mrs.

Adams paused. "By then the supernatural events in the Pelican had become the natural.

"Some years later I sold the restaurant in order to retire, but from all I hear, the ghost is still there. When my grandchildren come to visit me, I often take them out to dinner at the Black Pelican, and, invariably, my grandson will say, *This is so cool! We're going to the restaurant with the ghost.*"

. . . . . .

The Black Pelican is open year-round, except for Christmas and Thanksgiving. It is located at 3848 N. Virginia Dare Trail.

THE GHOSTLY LODGER
Roanoke Island Inn, Manteo, North Carolina

. . . .

The Roanoke Island Inn is a picturesque refuge in the small coastal port of Manteo, home of the outdoor drama *The Lost Colony*. As you pass through a wide archway, you are greeted by the heavy fragrance of pittosporum and the welcoming vision of the inn itself. A large house, reminiscent of those in the Caribbean, it is framed by the cool shadows of a giant live oak, and on the gallery porch above your head a ceiling fan turns lazily. Three dip nets for catching blue crabs hang on the wall of the inn. There is something timeless about this place, so that your first impression is of entering a quiet sanctuary safe from the cares of the world. The ghost here must feel that way too.

More than a century old, this house had been small when its first owners, Asa Jones and his wife, Martha, built it back in the 1860s. With each generation it grew larger. Now in the hands of architect John Wilson, a great-great-grandson of Asa Jones, the house has again doubled in size. Wilson, an islander, decided to redecorate it and open part of it as the Roanoke Island Inn.

In the entrance is a large central lighting fixture of intertwining cattails beautifully crafted of bronze, and spreading above it is a gloriously painted faux sky. A young North Carolina artist spent weeks depicting this airy cerulean world. It seems as real as the crystal vase full of fresh mint that sits nearby ready to lend pungency to a guest's glass of lemonade. Books fill the shelves on either side of the fireplace, and you sense that you will find this a place of spiritual renewal and peace.

Ada, the innkeeper, is waiting to greet you. You will know Ada Hadley by her long dark hair and her unusual accent. She came to Manteo from the island of Newfoundland, and when she talks about the fierce storms in her homeland, as those who live on islands often do, her storms in Newfoundland are an impressive blend of tropical hurricane and blizzard "bringing snow as high as the stove pipe."

For Ada, strange events began happening in her new island home right after her arrival.

"I was taking care of Mr. Wilson's grandfather on the second floor one night when I saw the figure of a huge man standing in the hall right in front of me. I saw his body and the shadowy features of his face, and he was looking straight through me! So terrified was I that I threw up my hands and pled the covering blood of Jesus, and then I flew down the stairs."

On another occasion Ada was sitting talking to Remie Lane, a friend of hers who lives here at the inn, when she heard a loud crash. She ran downstairs and on the floor found a vase filled with flowers that had been hurled across the room. Miraculously, the crystal was unbroken. "As we were picking up the flowers and mopping up water, we heard another sound, this time of glass shattering. It was a second vase, but this one had broken into many pieces.

"A day soon afterward I heard a sound upstairs in one of the bedrooms while I was upstairs cleaning. I knew which room it was and went in immediately. This was the room in which Mr. Roscoe Jones's wife died. The window had just *opened* of its own accord and the wind was blowing the curtains straight out. There was no good my reporting it to Mr. Wilson because everyone in the house knows the story of the ghost. The ghost was a member of the Wilson family and his name is Roscoe."

Of course the question most people ask is, Why did Roscoe become a ghost? Roscoe had been postmaster for many years in Manteo. Until he received a pink slip from the U.S. Postal Service, it had never occurred to him that he wouldn't be postmaster there for the rest of his life. He would not accept that losing his job could happen when there was a change of admin-

A ghostly former owner of the Roanoke Island Inn refuses to leave. It is such a lovely place, who can blame him?

istration in Washington. He wouldn't listen when his family told him it was "just politics." To him it was more than unfair to replace him; it was the greatest humiliation of his life.

A tall, slightly stoop-shouldered man with pale blue eyes, close-cropped gray hair, and a sober countenance, Roscoe Jones turned in his key at the post office and walked down Fernando Street. Rounding the curve that neared the water, he stopped in front of the house where he lived with his wife and family and stood staring at its entrance. He knew that this would be his final look at its exterior and he wanted to savor it. His eyes traveled over to the vines and lingered on the roses he had planted that climbed up to the gallery porch. He knew almost to the day each year when he could walk out the front door in the morning and see the first dewy buds of the season. For a moment he stopped and inhaled their fragrance.

Towering above him was the steep-pitched "bonnet roof" with eight dormer windows that he and his wife, "Miss Essie," had added on. It had been just right for their four children. He loved everything about this house, and he would never want to leave it.

He thought of the many times he had come home here after a day of supervising people on the mail routes and watching his two clerks to see that they obeyed regulations. His life would never be the same. Those faceless men in Washington who took his job away from him didn't know what a wicked thing it was to dismiss a man this way. He would never be able to look anyone in the eye again.

Without speaking to his wife or the other members of his family, former postmaster Roscoe Jones mounted the stairs to the second floor and went into his room. When his wife called him for supper, he did not appear. In fact no matter how the rest of the family called or cajoled, Roscoe never came down the stairs again in the presence of his family for the rest of his life. Mrs. Jones left a plate of food for him on a table, and he would come down late at night and take it upstairs to eat.

A few years later Roscoe died, and not long afterward the figure of a man in a postal uniform began to be seen leaving the house or entering the front door. Sometimes people downstairs would turn their head just in time to see a tall, shadowy, stooped man ascending the stairs.

"It's the postmaster. This house was his home and he just doesn't want to leave, is the way I try to explain it," says Ada. "His ghost has also closed the door of a room while I am working in it and not only startled me but became a bother. I knew it could only be him and I was becoming irritated, so I started rebuking him, saying 'Go away, Roscoe. I can't play these games now.' I think it often works, but sometimes, after I pull a blind down, he will pull it back up several times until I speak quite sharply to him. Then he will stop."

"Do you mind such weird happenings?" asked a guest. "No, not in the daytime," said Ada. "It's the noises at night that bother me. Footsteps are sometimes heard by our guests in room no. 7. Last week a lady was here and she asked me who was staying above her. She kept hearing the footsteps of someone walking back and forth, back and forth above her in a room we have never rented. It is only a storage area, and we think that end of the attic was part of Roscoe's quarters. Somehow those footsteps are worse than his turning the radio on in room no. 3."

The playing of the radio has attracted the attention of housekeeping. Although the room has been unoccupied each time the night before and no one has been in it to clean, they often hear music or voices inside it in the morning. Owner John Wilson says, "I have never seen the ghost, but I do have reports of his activities from my housekeeping staff and sometimes from our guests."

It had been over a year since I talked with Ada, the innkeeper. She called today, and we talked for a few minutes. I started to ask how Roscoe, the ghost, was, but she spoke first, as if I would know just who she was talking about.

"He's showing himself some again," she said. "Takes these spells of not letting us know he's here and then he does something like he did two weeks ago. Came up behind my daughter and pushed her—not a soul around!"

. . . . . .

The Roanoke Island Inn is located at 305 Fernando Street. For information or reservations, phone 252-473-5511.

Edenton was the first colonial capital of North Carolina, and if the decision were to be based on quaintness, history, and beauty, it might still be the capital today. The enormous grant of land to the lord proprietor, the Earl of Granville, from the King of England extended from the Carolina coast east almost as far as Charlotte. Unfortunately, Francis Corbin, whom Granville chose to administer this vast expanse of land, was an arrogant fellow who soon managed to antagonize not only the colony's leaders but also two of its governors.

Corbin built the lavish Cupola House for himself about 1758. Instead of purchasing the lot on which it stood in the name of his benefactor, he disregarded his instructions and bought it in his own name. Surely if the ambience of a house is influenced by the personality of its first owner, something of that person's nature becomes some part of it. That is the way it may be with Cupola House, judging by the experiences of those who take care of it. But let us evaluate the gentleman for ourselves—enter Mr. Corbin.

As we join Francis Corbin in colonial Edenton, he is standing in front of a tall gilt mirror eying the press of his lace-trimmed shirt and appraising the cut of his coat. Both appear to please him, and the quality of his attire leaves no doubt that being a land agent is indeed a lucrative position. A discreet knock and we see a servant enter his dressing room.

"Sir, the Moravian delegation is here."

"Good. Tell them I shall be there shortly and offer them a glass of ale."

Sharp German traders though the Moravians were, Corbin was a step ahead of them. He had already heard from one of his western spies how much they wanted a certain large tract of land near the Yadkin River. Corbin smiled at the thought of his secret information that the Moravians were willing to pay considerably more than the price they had offered him. When Corbin met with them, his demand was double the land's worth. Lord Granville would get a paltry share of this sum, while the balance of the land agent's exorbitant price would line his own pockets. "But that is the way of the world," he said to himself, and that was the way Francis Corbin did business.

It took only a few years before the colonists, indignant about his dishonest practices, organized a posse of armed citizens to seize Corbin and force him to promise reforms in the land office. Corbin's behavior had not only lost him Granville's support in England but most of his own influence in the colony. He retained some in certain quarters, perhaps due to his marriage to a rich widow, but he was heartily disliked and no longer wielded power. Corbin stayed in the Cupola House when in Edenton until shortly before his death in 1767.

Ironically, the overbudget, elaborate home built by him is today a National Historic Landmark, a house museum, and one of North Carolina's architectural treasures.

Some say there is an eerie quality about this house. According to a lady who has done volunteer work for the Cupola House Association, "Sometimes events of a supernatural nature occur in the rooms of Cupola House making people who work there uneasy. Before a hurricane we always go over to prepare the house. We place rags under doors, close shutters, take portraits off walls and place them on the beds, or bring in flower pots. But often, after a storm passes, when we go over to unlock the house, we find the key will not open the door.

"It appears that someone is standing on the other side trying to hold the door tightly closed. Just as strange is to find the bed on the second floor with a 'butt print' on it—as if someone has been sitting there. This is unlikely because that room, and the furniture in it, is always kept roped off!"

Other strange events are described by another volunteer, a respected Edenton lady with a love for history. This is her story.

"A friend of mine, who has worked for a number of years for the His-

It's amazing how something within Cupola House seems to hold the door closed from the inside.

toric Edenton Association, and I received a warning that a hurricane was on the way. We immediately went to work upstairs in the second floor hallway of the Cupola House preparing for the storm. During our preparations we were both astonished to hear a piece of heavy furniture being dragged across the floor in the children's room at the rear of the house. We were alone in the house, and when we gathered enough courage to go to the back and enter the room, nothing had been moved!

"I had two other unsettling experiences. Again a hurricane was on the way, and leaving the Visitor Center, I carried a strong flashlight, a new one, and hurried over to Cupola House, mounting the stairs to the third floor.

"I was standing behind a round drum-type enclosure containing a stairway, and I thought I should go up and raise the windows in the cupola just a little so that the wind would go through them. As I went up the stairs, the new flashlight I had brought went out. Returning to the Visitor Center, I found a second flashlight, tested it, and walked back over there. As soon as I mounted the stairs, that flashlight, too, went out. I admit that I was very nervous this time. The third flashlight worked!

"But strange things often happened in that house when I was alone or even when I conducted tours. When the group was quiet for a moment, I would sometimes hear the rustle and swish of taffeta as if someone were walking past us in a long dress. This happened a number of times, and it never ceased to give me chill bumps. I always wondered if it was the four Bond sisters who, after the death of their mother, lived on in this house until they died.

"In addition to the soft rustling sounds of women's skirts — and I almost hate to mention this, but — occasionally I have had the most uncomfortable sensation of walking through cobwebs. I have felt them clinging stickily to my face or on my arms, and yet none were visible. Of course, the Cupola House is regularly cleaned. The volunteer, who prefers to remain un-named, adds, "I never mention such things as the cobwebs or the sounds of furniture moving if I am conducting a tour. You know how nervous some people are about ghosts and the like."

. . . . . .

Cupola House is located at 408 S. Broad Street. It is open daily for tours that leave from the Visitor Center at 108 N. Broad Street. Cupola House is a National Historic Landmark, highly esteemed for its architectural significance.

BLACKBEARD'S HOUSE
Hammock Street, Beaufort, North Carolina

. . . .

Beaufort is a quaint coastal village that probably still looks much the way it did in the early 1700s. Pirates strutting down these narrow streets today would be at home. The old houses are similar to those built in the Bahamas by early mariners, and Blackbeard, who knew the Bahamas well, must have liked this small town. When he returned from his piratical expeditions, he would sail the *Queen Anne's Revenge* through the old channel into Beaufort Harbor and anchor her there, ready to keep any rendezvous at Ocracoke. Then he would head for the house where he and his crew stayed—Hammock House, known to this very day for its bloody history.

A local girl knows the story well. We leaned against her shiny green sports utility vehicle and stared curiously at the white frame house, its roof extending the width of its narrow porch. In the year 2000 it was almost three centuries old.

"That is the house that was once Blackbeard's," she said. "My mother was a friend of the people who owned it, and when I was a child, I stayed here and saw the stains on the stairs myself.

"It's called Hammock House now, but years ago people called it the Old White House. In the early days it was a landmark for sailing ships. When sea captains sighted the house through their glasses, they would set their compasses by it and sail safely through the inlet and into the harbor." She knew her history well and relished telling it.

Captain Edward Teach would stare out those front windows and watch the harbor lest a British sloop catch him unawares. It has been almost three centuries, yet some townspeople say they still feel the presence of one of history's most wicked pirates when they are near this house. Others claim they have heard peals of raucous laughter and drunken shouts resounding from the place on stormy nights.

And who were the pirates who hung out here obeying the commands of the ferocious Blackbeard? As noxious a band of rogues as you'll ever meet. You've probably heard of most of them and their fate—John Rose Archer (the *Adventure*'s quartermaster), Thomas Miller, James Blake, Owen Roberts (the ship's carpenter from Wales), John Martin, Edward Salter, Richard Stiles, James White, and Captain Teach's most loyal man of all, "Black Caesar."

Here at Hammock House the pirates entertained other buccaneers from along the coast unaware that these revelries would be their last. In the fall of 1718 it would not be long before Blackbeard's crew would stand on a gallows at Williamsburg, Virginia, and feel the hemp of the hangman's noose rough against their necks. When Captain Edward Teach was not preying upon wealthy pilgrims bearing expensive gifts to Mecca or seizing cargo vessels off the Atlantic and many another coast, the fishing village of Beaufort was one of his favorite retreats. He and his crew relaxed here following their voyages, for during the cold winter months even the hardiest of pirates were often reluctant to go "on account," their term for thievery on the high seas. This story, which came down through the townsfolk, is about just such a time. It is also about a lovely but rebellious local girl, Anne Gray, the pirate chieftain's sweetheart.

Blackbeard was on his way back to Beaufort from Philadelphia. As usual, he and his crew had enjoyed a bit of revelry at the Swede's place, a tavern at Marcus Hook, Pennsylvania, run by a woman called "the Swede." After leaving her place, Captain Teach and his crew spent several days along the Delaware Capes swapping stories with other pirate friends. But that was behind Teach now, and as his ship, the *Queen Anne's Revenge*, drew nearer to the Outer Banks, the pirate chief eagerly awaited the warm embrace of his current sweetheart, Anne Gray. She would be waiting for him at Hammock House in Beaufort and pleased she would be with his gifts.

As always, he brought back an ample amount of gold from ships he had seized and from the sale of stolen cargo in the port cities of Boston, New York, and Philadelphia.

Opening a woman's trunk on the day before he reached Beaufort, Blackbeard gloated over the contents. He had no recollection of the lady who had once owned it, nor how she had died. The other pirates could have what they wanted for their wives or sweethearts, but only after Anne had first choice, he thought. His fingers stroked dresses made of silk and cloth of gold from wealthy women who had turned them over gladly—in exchange for their lives. A few had been reluctant to cooperate and were now at the bottom of the sea. Others, more sensible, were at least admiring the scenery on some deserted island, but whose fault was that? Surely not his. His mind went back to Anne, her beautiful long brown hair in ringlets around her forehead and her smooth fair skin.

Why, he might even marry her some day. He certainly had nothing against the institution. Hadn't he already proven that by marrying a dozen women, or was it more? Stroking his beard, he tried to recall. Why did they always believe him so readily when he said, "I'm a single man"? Well, women always believe what they want to, he thought, smiling to himself.

Perhaps he should go ahead and propose to her now. It was really nothing to him, and while he was away it might keep her out of mischief, like the arms of another man. With that thought came a stab of jealousy, and he muttered various threats of what he would do if he ever caught her in the arms of some bloke. "I'll run the rascal through who touches her," he said to himself. As for Anne? It was better not to think what he would do to the soft flesh of that young lady. By now it was late afternoon. The wind and the weather had been with him all the way down the coast and he was several days earlier than his sweetheart expected. What a fine surprise it would be for her.

Back in Beaufort, at almost that same moment, Anne heard a knock at the back door of Hammock House and, opening it, saw her father. As usual, he began pleading with her to come home.

"Anne, you don't know how we worry about you, girl. These men are

A Beaufort girl says she once saw bloodstains on the wall of this house—bloodstains that have reappeared at intervals since Blackbeard murdered a young man on the stairs.

bad'uns. Your mother and I fear for you when we hear how they treat women and when we think of you with a ruffian the likes of Blackbeard."

Now Anne really lost her temper. "Go away! You and mama are going to ruin my life. That ruffian, as you call him, has said he is going to make a fine lady of me. You'll see!"

"You ain't learned a bit 'a sense, Anne. Unless you turn your back on this wild life, the wages of sin may be death, as the Good Book says!"

"Oh, so now he's going to kill me, is that it?" She stamped her foot. "He wouldn't dare!"

"I didn't say that. I'm just afraid you'll bring it on yourself, girl, by keeping such bad company. It's not too late to come back home and back to God—before you wind up in a pine box." There were tears in his eyes.

"You can't scare me. Don't you know things have changed since you were young? If you ever were!" she said, pushing him out and slamming the door. Then she leaned back against it, her heart pounding hard. Why didn't the old man leave her alone? This time he had really upset her more than she wanted him to know. What if he were right?

She admitted to herself that she was beginning to fear Blackbeard and several of the men in his crew, but the thought of telling the pirate chieftain that she wanted to leave was a terrifying one. She had seen his rages. What would he do? She glanced at the beautiful emerald bracelet on her wrist. Sometimes she felt like a rabbit in a trap. She needed to do something to calm herself and give her an opportunity to think, so she did what she always did at such times. She filled her pockets with pieces of bread and went out to feed the gulls. She loved the gulls, and they were used to her coming to feed them each day. By the time she had tossed the last piece in the air, she had made up her mind. She wanted to go home.

Yes, that was what she must do. Blackbeard and his crew were not due back yet, but something inside her was saying—go. Go now. Should she leave that very day? Heaven knows she wanted to, but her pride made her refuse her father the satisfaction of seeing her return home a few hours after he had left Hammock House. Anne got into bed and began to cry bitterly when she remembered the tears in her father's eyes. She knew in her heart that her parents loved her, and she caught a glimpse of her own past foolishness as it vanished.

Meanwhile, a short distance from Beaufort, Blackbeard's large hands with the thick black hair on the back raised a spy glass, and he stared out from under his bushy brows at the familiar white house. He would soon be there. No large ships were anchored at the Beaufort dock today, only a few fishing boats. Breathing a sigh of satisfaction, he set his compass by the house, more out of habit than anything else. He knew this inlet so well he could run it blindfolded.

At the house Anne was already up and dressed. She ate a bowl of porridge, and then, as she began packing her clothes, she heard a knock at the back door. Was it her father? She hoped so, for then she would go back with him. She called down, "Come in," and heard footsteps mount the stairs. To her surprise it was Samuel, the young farmer and fisherman who had once given her a present of a ring—a ring with the tiniest of stones but all he could afford. When Blackbeard had seen it, he roared with laughter and pitched it over the side of his ship. Reaching into a chamois bag at his waist, he said, "Hold out your hand," and she saw a glint of green and gold as he dropped a ring with an enormous emerald into her outstretched palm.

Now, as she looked at Samuel whom she had not seen in months, she remembered the ring he had wanted her to have. He was like her parents, she thought, content with the simplest of things—to be back from the sea, to be in his own little house and in church of a Sunday. She was surprised at how happy she was that he was here.

"You know I still want to marry you. Do you really love that man, Anne?" asked Samuel. With his finger he tilted up her chin and looked deep into her eyes.

She leaned against him and cried like a child. "No, Sam. No. Sometimes I'm so afraid of him."

"Well why did you come to his house then?"

"Because of the jewelry and fine clothes he gave me. My friends in Beaufort were impressed when they saw Blackbeard admired me."

"Didn't your mother warn you about him?"

"Yes, but I thought she was jealous and angry because I wouldn't be there to help her—that she didn't want me to have a life of my own."

"Oh, no, Anne. That's not so. She wants you to have a fine life, not a life of being knocked around. In town they say they saw you with bruises on your face and arms."

"That is true, but he swore he would never hit me again."

"A man who strikes a woman once will do it again!"

Her lips trembled and she looked down.

"Anne," persisted Samuel, "this man murders innocent people and gives you the jewels warm from their bodies. Is that what you want to wear?"

A blush colored her face. "Oh, no! No!" She walked restlessly around the room and toward the window. He followed.

"Just tell me one thing. Do you love me Anne?"

"Yes, but when it began you were away on a whaling trip."

"I was coming back and with money honest-earned," said Samuel.

Anne looked out toward the waterfront and gave a sudden start.

"What is the matter?" he asked.

"He's back! Oh Sam, he's coming now!"

And there he was. Striding up toward the house came the tall, swaggering figure that seaports throughout the world knew as the most terrifying pirate of them all—Blackbeard.

"I'll hide you," she cried out desperately and caught at Samuel's arm. He pulled away. "I can defend myself," he said, his hand on his knife. "He's alone, and I'm going down to meet him."

Unable to stop the young fisherman, Anne gave a little scream of protest and, turning, dropped to the ground through a raised window at the back of the house. Samuel was halfway down the stairs when the front door opened. The brawny, broad-shouldered figure filled the doorway, and for an instant Blackbeard stared up at him. Then the pirate let fly a stream of the most awful curses as, eyes blazing, he charged up the stairs like an enraged bull elephant. With one sweep of his cutlass, the pirate struck, and Samuel fell across the stairs mortally wounded. A crimson stream spurted from the slash across his throat onto the stairs.

"People who have lived in that house say they have often tried to wash away the stains where Blackbeard killed the young man, but splotches dark as dried blood return. That is just what I saw years ago," said the girl.

"And what of Anne Gray? They say that Anne was found washed ashore near Beaufort. She had been stabbed to death and thrown into the ocean. Villagers believed that Blackbeard himself had killed her. And gossip in the town had it that even before her body was found, *Anne's emerald bracelet and ring were being worn by another—a new girl who had taken the pirate's fancy!*"

Today, near the water, the gulls still soar and squawk, "cree . . . cree . . . cree," the same cry they made the day they swooped down over Anne while she lay upon the beach—a poor, foolish girl who would hear them no more.

· · · · · ·

The house that Captain Edward Teach made his headquarters for a time is now a private residence. Although there is a sign in front to identify it, the house is not open to the public.

THE PHANTOM SHIP
Beaufort, North Carolina

. . . .

I t was the last of August, and Captain John Sabiston's ship was back
in the busy port of Beaufort. This was not the first time Sabiston
had noticed the girl among the crowd of villagers who came down
to meet the ships when they sailed into Beaufort. She was taller
than most of the women and held herself proudly. Her chestnut
hair was streaked gold by the sun, and he liked the way she moved—with
grace and vitality—a look of eager anticipation on her face.

As he walked along the dock, he found himself headed directly toward
her and passed so close that his large duffel bag brushed the sky blue cham-
bray of her dress.

"Pardon me, ma'am," he said.

"It's quite all right, sir." Her voice was breathless. "Have you seen Robert Chadwick?"

"He was one of the first off."

"Then he is already on his way home," she said, a quick smile lighting up
her face. "Thank you," she said and, turning away, walked quickly through
the crowd. An unusually attractive young woman, thought the captain,
who told himself Chadwick was a lucky fellow. But marriage and the sea
don't always mix, and Sabiston reflected that it was not for him. As his
friends had so often told him, "You are married to the sea and your ship."
He had heard that, in Greece, a man taking command of a vessel for the
first time would hang a crown of laurel leaves on the ship. It was the custom in that country for the bride to wear a crown of laurel upon the exchange of her wedding vows.

Captain Sabiston was approaching thirty and had been captain of his own vessel for a year. This morning as he looked about him, he saw his friend Captain Ireland, and the two men greeted each other warmly. Ireland asked where he would be staying, and when Sabiston admitted he had no idea, Ireland invited him to be his houseguest. Since he would be in port a week or more while his schooner was unloading and preparing for her next voyage, Sabiston accepted gladly.

Captain Ireland's wife, Jane, was an accomplished musician as well as a good cook, and Captain Sabiston's visit promised to be even more pleasant than he expected as he and Ireland, whom he had known but casually, discovered shared interests. Both were students of botany and enjoyed taking long walks together while Sabiston acquired considerable information about the plant life of the southern coast.

The second night Sabiston was in port, Mrs. Ireland had a party, and for the first time Sabiston met many of the townspeople socially rather than primarily as customers for his cargo or as merchants who stocked his vessel with supplies for the next voyage. Chadwick was there with the girl who had been looking for him at the dock, and they joined the captain as he stood listening to Mrs. Ireland play the the harpsichord.

"I am glad to see you again, Captain," said Chadwick. "I think from my conversation and letters to her that Mattie here already knows our paths have crossed in various ports. Mattie, this is Captain Sabiston." Sabiston bowed courteously yet felt strangely ill at ease and inwardly blamed his awkwardness upon his months at sea with only the rough men of a ship's crew for company.

"How do you do, Mrs. Chadwick."

Mattie looked surprised, and Chadwick spoke quickly.

"I'm sorry, sir. I thought you knew I am unmarried. Mattie is my sister."

The captain gazed at her. "I see, and I am most happy to meet you ma'am.

"Beaufort is my home port," explained Chadwick, and I am always glad to put in here to see my sister and widowed mother. It was apparent that the captain was quite taken with Mattie, for he stood there staring at her with obvious approval and scarcely seemed to hear Chadwick's words. Mrs. Ireland noticed this with a woman's perception and, rising from the piano, whisked them away to seats at the dining room table. She placed the captain and Mattie on her right, and before long the two were engaged in animated conversation.

During the following weeks Mattie joined Captain Sabiston and Captain Ireland on their daily nature walks, and at night Sabiston often called upon her at the Chadwick home. All ideas of laurel wreaths as the symbol of a captain's marriage to his ship were soon forgotten. Captain Sabiston proposed, and he and Mattie were married before he went on his next voyage back to Baltimore. On these trips his ship was filled with hides, fish, tar, pitch, and turpentine from Carolina as well as tea, spices, rope, and cloth that had arrived in the Beaufort port from abroad.

John and Mattie were happy together, their marriage blessed with children, and the years passed quickly. Each time Sabiston's three-masted schooner would sail into the harbor on its return from Baltimore, he would anchor in the same place. Mattie could see it from her window, and, scarcely able to contain her happiness, she would run down to the dock to greet him.

When his ship, the *Esmeralda*, was due in port, she would hurry to open the drapes each morning and stare out at the harbor, hoping to see its sails with the salmon-tinted glow of the sunrise behind them. And then one September dawn, it was there. From her window she saw the vessel lying at anchor, the sun glinting on its brass fittings, the ship's sleek lines a joy to behold. Her husband stood beside the mizzenmast looking toward the house as if he knew she was at the window. She saw him raise an arm and wave. Mattie's heart quickened within her. Snatching up a small shawl, she opened the window and waved it, but he did not wave again.

Dressing quickly, she hurried down to the dock to greet him. But to her amazement the schooner was not there, nor was it anywhere in the harbor. As her eyes searched the waterfront, she saw her brother just stepping over on the dock from his own vessel. His lean, tanned face was grave, and immediately she knew something was wrong.

He put his arm around her, "Mattie, I don't know how to break the news to you, but I must. John's ship went down in a storm."

"No! I just saw it!" cried Mattie. "It was right in the place where he always anchors. The ship I saw was John's. Where has it gone?"

"You couldn't possibly have seen the *Esmeralda*, sister, or John either. We were separated during a nor'easter, and near dusk when the wind abated I saw him through my glasses to the south of us. We set our sails to overtake him, but the sea was still rough and the waves towered above my ship. I saw the *Esmeralda* rise from a trough to the crest and then fall back on its side as if felled by some monstrous hand. It sank so rapidly no one could help them."

"But his ship—it was out in the harbor this morning in its usual place."

"Mattie, you can't have seen it. The *Esmeralda* will never anchor in Beaufort Harbor again," her brother said sadly. Mattie began to sob wildly and then to berate the sea.

"Why did the sea snatch him away? I hate you! I hate you, I . . . hate . . . you!" she cried out looking across the water.

"Hush, Mattie. Hush," said her brother holding her to him until her cries died away and became soft anguished moans.

"But how could I have seen his ship this morning?"

"My dear, you can only have seen a phantom ship sailed by a crew from another world."

"No. It was John," said Mattie Sabiston. She took a deep breath and straightened her shoulders. "He came back for one last good-bye," she said quietly and walked toward the house.

THE GHOST OF FORT MACON
Morehead City, North Carolina

. . . .

If you were one of the men on the staff of Fort Macon, how would you like to have a ghost single you out as his favorite ranger? That is exactly what seems to be happening to Paul Branch, historian at one of North Carolina's most historic forts, a fort upon which he has lavished hour upon hour of his life as he researches and records its fascinating history.

Branch's book, *Fort Macon*, should not be judged on the basis of accounts of the number of battles fought at the fort, heroic episodes during the shelling or any overwhelming victories. Instead, it is the story of this fort's vital location and a change that occurred here in modern warfare as revolutionary as the development of the Winchester rifle. It was only the second time in history that rifled cannons would be used to breach the walls of a fort. This scoring or rifling inside the barrel of the guns made them considerably more accurate and more deadly than ever before.

But back to our story of Officer Branch's ghostly admirer. It was early spring of 1861 when a farm boy named Ben Combs was considering leaving Goldsboro, North Carolina, to join the Confederate army. His father saw no sense to it at all and told him so.

"You don't know nothin' about soldierin', boy; you're a farmer. You got patience with animals, and you got an eye for plowin' a straight row. But lately you stand around doin' nothin' but chewin' tobacco and lookin' off in the distance. I figure you got to be doin' some powerful thinkin' because you movin' so slow."

"I ain't fast like you, Pa, because I ain't used to making decisions yet, but they'll learn me that in the . . ."

"Go ahead and say it. You mean the army."

"Yes. I'm thinkin' that I want to jine up, Pa. The Yankees are going to invade our state, and the boys in Goldsboro are forming companies and offering them to the governor."

"Your ma's not goin' to take to this, but I see you got your mind set on it," said his father. And "jine up" Ben Combs did. Many of the soldiers from both North and South were like him. They were store clerks, shoemakers, teachers, sailors, fishermen, and farmboys who didn't know what soldiering was all about. Ben heard that President Lincoln had asked the governor of North Carolina to send troops to attack South Carolina because they had seceded. He knew North Carolina wasn't about to do such a thing, and they wouldn't 'til the bad place froze over.

Ben was soon at Fort Macon with the Goldsboro Volunteers and the Goldsboro Rifles. He knew many of the boys that were already there, and they regarded it as a great adventure, the most exciting thing that had ever happened in their lives. None of them had any idea of the desperate struggle that lay ahead. Everyone was digging like crazy, hurrying to level the sand dunes that stood between Fort Macon and the water so they would have a clear field to fire on the Yankees when they landed to try to take the fort. Ben found the digging hard work but no harder than working with his pa on the farm, and his spirits, like those of the other men, were high.

On the night of May 21 news came that North Carolina too had finally seceded from the Union, and that brought on a wild demonstration. Men shouted and cheered, and at the end of the announcement they all began singing "Dixie" and the "Old North State Forever"—"While I live I will cherish, protect, and defend her. Hurrah! Hurrah! The Old North State forever," sang Ben. He knew he would protect North Carolina from northern invasion even at the risk of his life.

He enjoyed learning the military life at the fort, reveille at sunrise, drills, target practice, where he once got "best shot," and the talk with his comrades about how they were going to defend Morehead City. He had already decided that when the Yankees were defeated and the war was over, he would like to stay in the army and be stationed here at Fort Macon. It

If a door closes quietly behind you in an empty hall or you see three shadows but only two park rangers here at Fort Macon, don't be disturbed. It's only Ben. (Photograph courtesy of Fort Macon)

was never lonely or dull like the farm at Goldsboro had been, and he enjoyed watching the ships come and go in the harbor. He often walked along or sat upon the wall staring northeast toward Beaufort or west toward the harbor and Morehead city anticipating the direction the Yankees would come from.

When the attack finally came in the spring of 1862, Ben worked desperately to mount a special cannon with a ten-inch mortar shell. A fuse was cut too long, and the shell rolled right toward him. The farmboy who had never been faced with a danger like this before did not move quickly enough to get out of the way—he froze. Finally he ran, but it was too late; the shell seemed to pursue him like some evil demon, and when it finally caught up with him, it exploded in his back, shattering his rib cage. There was nothing the fort surgeon could do, for the broken ribs had punctured his lungs. During the several days that he lived on, Ben's pain was excruciating. He thought about home. None of the boys back in Goldsboro had ever told him war could be like this.

After the Civil War was over, the Outer Banks lapsed back into their quiet, almost prehistoric isolation. There was a flurry of activity at Fort Macon during the Spanish-American War, but it was followed by long years when the fort lay abandoned in a state of decay. Its brick sidewalks were crumbling, the parade ground was overgrown with brush, and its walls were shrouded with vines. The fort fell prey to vandals.

When Officer Paul Branch arrived at Fort Macon in June of 1981, he became fascinated with its history. He had heard rumors of the fort's ghost but paid little heed to them until strange incidents began happening to him. He soon found out that no one wanted to be asked to work alone inside the fort at night. He thought it ridiculous until one evening, after he had been completing some research in his office and was ready to leave, he turned the knob of the door only to find himself locked in from the outside. This was one of a series of incidents that caused him to regard the story of the ghost more seriously.

Numerous times at night when the fort is deserted and someone is alone in the office or two officers are working together, the clap of a door firmly closing is heard. Since only one man was killed in battle here, whenever a particularly incredible incident happens, the men at the fort have fallen into the habit of calling the ghost by the name of "Ben."

Probably one of the strangest experiences happened to Ranger Branch himself. He was out on the drill ground in the center of the fort on a bright sunny day and happened to notice two of the men assigned to the post sitting on the wall. He had first noticed them because of the long shadows their figures cast. A moment later he glanced back at them, trying to recall their names. They still sat there, but this time, below them on the wall and in approximately the same position, was a third shadow, also that of a man, but only the same two men were sitting on the wall above. Their positions were unchanged!

Men stationed at the fort say it is not unusual for objects customarily kept in one place to appear in some remote and bizarre spot. Doors have been known to close behind officers who were walking down a corridor when the headquarters building was empty. Once one of the officers saw the door to his own office close, although the hall outside the door was empty. Visitors touring the fort occasionally report strange experiences but Officer Branch says reassuringly that he has never known of the ghost harming anyone.

As dusk descends on Fort Macon in the year 2000, 139 years after North

Carolina seceded from the Union, you can hear the pounding of the surf just as the men did when they were stationed here in 1861 and 1862. If we listen attentively, is it possible to hear Ben Combs's ardent young voice raised in song just as it was the night the fort received the news of secession?

"While I live I will cherish, protect, and defend her. Hurrah! Hurrah! The Old North State forever." Ben had wanted to defend his state with all his heart.

So don't be startled when you visit Fort Macon if Ben's unseen hand closes the door behind you or if you count the officers and see an extra shadow figure on the wall. Like many of the men and women who serve at Fort Macon State Park today, you may soon believe that Ben's spirit is still here.

· · · · · ·

Fort Macon State Park is the only state park with a military fort. It is also one of North Carolina's top attractions and has one of the highest number of visitors of any North Carolina state park. For information, phone 252-726-3775.

Bellamy Mansion, Wilmington, North Carolina

. . . .

When Dr. John Bellamy locked the front door of his impressive house behind him in 1862, he was uncertain whether he and his wife and nine children would ever see it again. But there was to be a future for his magnificent house, although not one the owner would like. Dr. Bellamy knew that Fort Fisher, which protected the port city of Wilmington, would inevitably become the prime target of a Union attack. The city was already changing from a sleepy river town to the South's busiest port, its streets and boarding houses overflowing with the rowdy crews of American and British blockade runners.

One of the first ships to run the Union blockade was a side-wheeler, the *Kate*, which brought a large cargo of supplies from Nassau. The city received it with cheers, unaware that death was a passenger on board. Members of the *Kate*'s crew, infected with yellow fever, carried the disease into the city, where it immediately went on a house-to-house rampage.

For the people of Wilmington, 1862 was the worst of all years. Each day, wagons clattered along the streets, their drivers collecting the bodies of yellow fever victims for mass burials. As if this were not enough, there was also the threat of a Yankee invasion—a threat that persisted until January 1865, when, as Dr. Bellamy had anticipated, Fort Fisher finally fell, and General Joseph Hawley commandeered the Bellamy Mansion as headquarters for the Union occupation of Wilmington.

When the war was over, the Bellamy family returned to Wilmington, and Mrs. Bellamy called upon General Hawley's wife to inquire courteously as to the date they might expect to move back into their home. Mrs. Hawley drew herself up and with great haughtiness declared that she had no intention of moving out. Hearing that the general would not return his house and property, the doctor traveled to Washington and obtained a personal pardon from President Andrew Johnson. The Bellamy family was permitted to move back into the house late in the summer of 1865.

Recently this impressive twenty-two-room mansion was restored and opened to the public. Much of the beautiful original molding, crafted by skilled slave artisans and freedmen under the direction of a young Connecticut draftsman, may still be seen. The Bellamys' prized rosewood William Knabe piano is one of the pieces of the mansion's original furniture on display.

Curator Jonathan Noffke looks around him and says thoughtfully, "This is a house of many legends. One story is that if you happen to be here at midnight you may hear a booted Yankee soldier dash up the front steps."

A visitor to the city says, "If you are passing by and gaze at the dark shuttered eyes of the white columned-old mansion, it doesn't take a sixth sense to know that *something is really here.*

"This house has a long and well-deserved reputation for being haunted." Curator Noffke says, "There is no single apparition in a particular place. Here it is in different places. It seems to move around." He compares the ambience of the Bellamy Mansion to that of the grand houses of William Faulkner's stories. "But of course you want to know what ghosts are here," says Noffke. "I have had no personal experience with any, but when they were filming a movie here, prior to the 1993 and 1994 restoration, quite a startling story was told me by the location scout.

"He and the director were in the library looking through some old papers that were blackened by a fire which occurred here in 1972 and this is what he said.

" 'We had locked the door behind us and were completely alone in the house when suddenly we heard the heavy front door open and slam shut with a loud bang. A cold blast of air rushed *through the closed door* up the stairs and into the library, where we were working. Our papers sailed through the air in every direction.

"'Within seconds, we were out of there and racing down the steps when we heard the library door slam shut over our heads. That was followed by an angry pounding on it as if someone had been ejected and was furiously attempting to get back in. We ran down another flight of stairs to the ground floor beneath the house.'

"I gathered they were very frightened," smiled the curator. "But let me mention the third floor of the mansion. It is not only physically very different from the rest of the house, but so is its atmosphere. People walking up from the second to the third floor often mention being uncomfortable on the stairs and feeling ill at ease upstairs. Visitors who claim psychic sensibilities are plainly eager to leave that floor. The third floor contains the bedrooms that once belonged to the nine Bellamy children.

"As for people seeing things," says the curator, "it does not happen up there. The second floor is where it happens. Volunteers report that when they are locking up they glimpse the bottom of a trouser leg or the flutter of a long skirt moving out of the room just ahead of them. It is as if someone was just leaving. I've never had any of these experiences myself, but I serve as a clearinghouse for them.

"Whatever ghosts are reported to inhabit the mansion seem to be non-threatening, reticent presences. A strange incident occurred some years back," the curator continued. "A film crew was driving by, and they reported seeing an elderly couple staring out a window on the third floor. Others have also seen them. The pair stand in the double window behind the balcony and gaze out over Market Street.

"Hostesses here have had their own experiences, such as being in a room and feeling that they were not alone. On one occasion I was talking to a group of volunteers, giving them pointers, when one of the volunteers named Kim suddenly cried out. I looked at her startled.

"'Pardon me, sir,' she said, 'but I just saw a figure standing behind you looking over your shoulder!'"

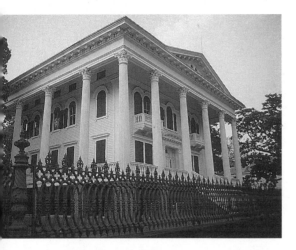

The Bellamy Mansion has the reputation of being Wilmington's most haunted house. (Photograph courtesy of the Bellamy Mansion)

The house and the history-making events that have taken place here provide a popular background for Civil War reenactments and, more than once, an encounter with something more. Jim Morgan, a Wilmington reenactor, and a group of other men playing the part of Union soldiers were to spend the night in the Bellamy Mansion, where Union soldiers lived and slept during the war. Morgan's son, Robert, persuaded his father to let him go along. "I've heard stories that things happen in that house, Dad, and I would like to spend the night there," said the youth.

The fact that his son was eager to experience something supernatural irritated his father, who was a thoroughgoing skeptic, but he consented, believing that Robert would at least absorb some Wilmington Civil War history. During the night Mr. Morgan was awakened by peals of laughter and sounds suspiciously like pillow fighting from the third floor. He immediately thought Robert might be involved, so he rose from his pallet on the parlor floor where the reenactors lay sleeping and hurried up the stairs. Sweeping the beam of his flashlight through the rooms, he discovered that they were empty. No one was sleeping on the third floor. Continuing his search, he finally found his son with some friends, all lying peacefully asleep, on the second floor.

Returning to the parlor, Morgan lay back down still wondering about the laughter he had heard. Then, tired from the day's activities, he dropped off to sleep. But during the early morning hours his rest was broken once more. He waked up to feel the pressure of heavy boots striding roughly across his body. Outraged, Morgan was convinced that some of his re-enactor buddies were playing a dumb joke on the rest of them. The sleepy, angry shouts of his comrades and their imprecations began to fill the air. To his astonishment Morgan saw the shadowy figures of Union soldiers walking over the sleeping bodies of the reenactors.

He and his comrades, now thoroughly awake, began to strike out at them. Two of the reenactors turned on flashlights, determined to see who the practical jokers were and teach them a good lesson. When someone hit the parlor light switch, which illuminated the entire room, and found it empty, the reenactors fell silent. With awestruck faces, they looked around them. The dark figures had vanished. Men, with hands raised to strike, found themselves facing only each other, and sheepishly they lowered their fists. Everyone lay down again, but there was little sleep to be had that night for Morgan. Listening to men turn restlessly from one side to the other, he couldn't go back to sleep, and as he thought about what had happened, he had a queasy feeling. Would they return? The thought of those tall, shadowy figures made his flesh creep!

Finally he dozed off, and the next thing he knew it was light. His son was leaning over him, a hand on his shoulder.

"Hey, dad! wake up," Robert said. "Wow! What a wasted night. This house doesn't have any ghosts." Robert was ready to go home.

The reenactment went on until the following afternoon, and no one mentioned the events of the night before. But later they began to discuss plans for another reenactment, and invariably someone would comment upon how hard it was to sleep in old houses. They questioned each other cautiously, no one wanting to risk ridicule. Several finally admitted that the place gave them nightmares and mentioned soldiers walking over them while they slept!

Many longtime residents of Wilmington, and some of the staff who work at the Bellamy Mansion, believe it to be the most haunted house in the city.

. . . . . .

The Bellamy Mansion Museum is open year-round for touring. It is located at 503 Market Street. For information, phone 910-251-3700.

THE HAUNTED WILMINGTON LIBRARY
New Hanover County Public Library, Wilmington, North Carolina

· ·

The new library in Gainesville, Georgia, has a ghost, and when I wrote a story about it for my book *Georgia Ghosts*, it never occurred to me that I would soon discover a second haunted library.

Beverly Tetterton, of the North Carolina Room, tells of more than one ghost said to haunt the New Hanover County Public Library. Spectral visitors have been reported at two locations of the library—the old armory, first in use as the library during the Civil War, and the building where the library is currently located. The library's present location was formerly the site of a wealthy family's private home. Books donated to the library by the family are now housed in the North Carolina Historical Collection. Here is where much, but not all, of the ghostly activity takes place.

Could a ghost have arrived along with the old books?

Mrs. Tetterton, a former employee at Colonial Williamsburg, has transferred her enthusiasm for history to Wilmington. Her interest in pirates, secret tunnels to the river from some of the historic houses, and the network of storm sewage tunnels (some high enough for a man to stand up in) beneath the old city hint of years of high adventure!

But back to the supernatural. Mrs. Tetterton has had a number of experiences herself. "Some of them are just sounds. Sounds that only a librarian might be familiar with," she says—"like a patron shelving a book, pages being leafed back and forth as people do when they search through an index, file drawers being opened and closed. Some nights I have sat for hours at my desk, and all the time I could hear so much activity back there in the stacks! The sounds would begin as if someone were putting their elbows on a metal shelf to read or books were being placed with a thump on a shelf—yet I would know that the last person had left the library because I had just said good night to them.

"We have locked up at night and returned the next morning to find every drawer in the pamphlet file case unlocked and one or more left partially open!

"When we worked at the old library, the one that had the tall bushes around it and did not close until eight o'clock, we had a strict closing procedure. I would walk through the stacks with a co-worker and all over the building just to be sure no one was locked in accidentally. I walked the building myself, and so in my own mind I felt sure no one was there but the two of us. One night shortly after I began working there, we had been through the stacks and were walking near the circulation desk, which was on our left. Back down the hall were the stacks. We both saw a shadow move, and I said, 'Oh, there is someone still left in the building.'

"'We need to get out of here now,' my co-worker replied. 'Get your hat and pocket book, and let's go outside.' We were standing in front of the building breathless when I asked her, 'What was all that about?' and she answered, 'Didn't you know this building is haunted?' That was my introduction to the ghosts of the soldiers of the past—the Wilmington Light Infantry! The WLI were in that building during the time it was an armory."

Mrs. Tetterton thought she had left incidents of that sort behind her when they moved to the new library, but it seems they were here too.

"One day a patron came out of the stacks and up to me to report seeing a woman going around the corner of an aisle of shelves. She tried to catch up to tell her the library was closing when she faded and disappeared." Other sightings have been reported to her by library patrons, but Mrs. Tetterton prefers not to identify them. Sometimes that embarrasses people. "On separate occasions the apparition of a woman researcher was seen by two male patrons," says Mrs. Tetterton.

"The woman they described was very similar in appearance to a local historian we all knew and respected who died several years ago. One thing I love about being a librarian is assisting people with historical research. The problems they bring to me are never the same. The story I'm going to tell you illustrates that and is one of the most interesting experiences I've had since working in the library.

"I was sitting here at my desk one afternoon when a woman came in who was not a patron I knew. The first thing she said was, 'I'm so upset you must help me! I want to see all your ghost story files.'

"When I began I had no idea I was going to be drawn into the midst of a contemporary ghost story. She told me that the night before she had been waked up in the early morning hours by a ruckus out in the hall and had heard something very frightening. She stays in a lodging house in the middle of the historic district—an interesting old white house—one of the few with a second floor balcony.

"She went on to describe her experience, saying, 'I was sound asleep when I was awakened by noises and the sound of scuffling right outside my door. This was followed by a woman's imploring voice crying out, "Major Clark, don't do it! Please don't do that! Please, Major Clark. . . ." There was the crack of a shot and a scream. I heard the sound of something heavy being pulled to the top of the stairs, and as it was dragged down it went bump, bump, bump with a dull thud as it hit each stair. I knew it had to be a body, and I lay in bed petrified. I could hear it slide heavily across the floor toward the door of the downstairs hall. Then I heard the creak of the front door opening and the dragging noise resumed as if a weight was being pulled over the threshold and out onto the porch. Finally the door closed, and to my relief, I could hear no more.

"'The next morning when I awakened all was silent in the house, and immediately I went out my door to look in the hall. There was no reason to think anything unusual had happened. Nor were there signs of any disturbance. Somehow I became increasingly sure that this was not something that happened last night, but that it was an actual event that had happened in that house years ago. Someone must have heard all this before, and I am wondering if it is in your file of ghost story clippings?'

"I was not familiar with it, but I gave her the file and she searched. There

Several staffers have seen or heard a ghost at the New Hanover County Public Library.

was nothing there, and we had exhausted every possible source I knew of for her to check. The hour was drawing toward five o'clock, and I had a report to complete, so I tried a last resort to satisfy her that nothing had occurred. That is what I really believed. I suggested that she try the microfilm and look up the Wilmington newspaper for a hundred years ago yesterday. With this to keep her occupied, I went back to my desk and my work.

"I was surprised to see her return before long, her face pink with excitement.

"'Mrs. Tetterton, this is it—the next day, one hundred years after last night's date. Read this.' While I stood searching the microfilm, she pointed to a few lines at the very bottom of the page. There in the Wilmington paper was a three-line notice, and I read these words: 'Major Clark was found lying dead this morning at the foot of Orange Street.' Just that and no details as to how he met his death.

"'And where is the house you live in?' I inquired.

"'Orange Street,' she replied. 'I live at 413 Orange Street,' and now her face had turned chalk white. 'I know it happened in that house, for I heard it take place—Major Clark tried to kill someone and instead they killed him.'

"'I wish I could help you,' I said to her. This event was before the filing of death certificates in Wilmington, so there was no way to look up Major Clark and the cause of death. 'It could be either a Union or Confederate officer. Both were here during the Civil War.'

"'If anything else happens in the house may I come back?'

"'Of course, if you think there might be something in our files.'

"She turned. 'Mrs. Tetterton, you have been so helpful and seem to know so much about ghosts. . . . You do, don't you?'

"I started to say no and then thought of all the tales told to me by my Scandinavian grandmother—not to mention experiences working in haunted libraries. 'Well, perhaps you are right,' I admitted. 'If you discover any more information about the Major, do let me know.'"

. . . . . .

The New Hanover County Public Library is located at 201 Chestnut Street.

II

South Carolina

GHOST OF THE OLD FIREHOUSE
Myrtle Beach, South Carolina

. . . .

Broadway at the Beach, Restaurant Row, the Pavilion—visitors don't think of ghosts in connection with the glitter of the Grand Strand. The story of a tall, intelligent man, now prominent in Myrtle Beach civic life, may make us change our minds.

Former fireman John Simpson says, "I had an experience in the old firehouse that I will carry with me forever. It is immaterial to me whether anyone believes it or not."

"I was was stationed at the old firehouse on 13th Avenue," says John. "That station was an isolated place, not like the one we have now, and I'm glad. The building now serves as a warehouse for the city of Myrtle Beach.

"At the time, I worked nights, and the fireman who worked with me, B. J., was a friend of several years' standing, but we began to have a real disagreement over something that was happening. Night after night we would hear footsteps and then the sound of one of the bay doors being opened. We would rush out of our room to see who was doing it, but no one was ever there. The grounds around the station were clear of other buildings and bushes, so that if anyone was running away we would have seen him immediately.

"We first thought someone was playing tricks on us. The controls were electric. The buttons were on the inside, and you had to press one and hold it down to open the bay door. If you turned the button loose, the door would go back up. We would hear the sound of it descending and go out to check, only to find it suspended in midair. That means it was either stuck in place or someone whom we could not see was standing there holding the button down with an invisible finger.

"Then we looked for a way it could have jammed, perhaps something wedged in supporting it there, such as a piece of wood, but nothing was ever found. In the daytime the door worked fine. It would only descend at night. Some of us figured that we knew who was doing it, and I thought I was pretty sure who the ghost was. I thought of what I had heard all my life, that one reason people return to a place is because they have unfinished business to complete.

"Now there had been a man named Burns working outside the fire station connecting some electrical wires that led to the building. He got too close to a live wire, and they said that he was drawn toward that wire like a magnet. Someone looked out and there he was hanging among the wires. We tried to rescue him, and one of the strangest things was that although he was in the midst of a tangle of live wires that had not been shut off yet from the main line, not one of us working to rescue him was injured.

"Another thing we didn't understand was that this guy had been wiring buildings for some twenty years and never had a problem. They said he was an expert and had done some of the most dangerous jobs anyone could do. He took real pride in his work. How could his performing a simple task get him electrocuted? I believed he was back because he simply had not finished. He had begun the electrical work and died before completing what he set out to do. The ghost had to be this fellow named Burns.

"B. J. and I would hear that door creak as the ghost descended late at night, and both of us would hurry out of the bedroom to check. Although we never found a natural explanation for it, B. J. always said there was no such thing as a ghost being the cause.

"Then my friend B. J. died from a heart attack. One night a few weeks later I was shocked and frightened when I saw him standing right in the room with me just like he used to there at the fire station.

"He spoke quite clearly, saying, 'Johnny, I want to tell you that I believe your story about the other man who died here. I believe it now for reasons than I cannot explain to you because I am not in your world anymore.'

"I told a friend of mine about it who was present when B. J. appeared but neither he nor any of the other men saw or heard anything. He asked how I knew who it was.

"I told him I knew it was B. J. because I could see him clearly, but I couldn't say a word. I think I was being prevented from exposing him because he was speaking only to me.

"'What was he wearing?' someone asked, and I said he was wearing his fireman's uniform.

"The last thing I heard him say to me was, 'Let's go.' When he said, 'Let's go,' I'm looking like 'what does he mean?' Is he taking me with him? I don't need that! Or is he speaking to someone with him that I'm unable to see.

"But finally I put two and two together. Apparently B. J. was talking to a companion. My dead friend had come back to let me know that what I had witnessed and what he had so often disputed me about was the truth. He must have been speaking to the guy who had held his finger on the button that lowered the bay door. When he said, 'OK, let's go,' it was to his ghostly companion and not me. Realizing that, I breathed a deep sigh of relief, for I was not eager to accompany him!

"From that day on I felt comfortable when I was in the station by myself.

"That building of metal, wood, and brick still stands, shabbier with age. Sometimes I glance over at it when I pass and wonder if the two men are at peace. On the other hand, are they just waiting—waiting for someone else to occupy the building so they may roam it once more when the sun sets and the shadows cluster around it after dark?"

* * * * * *

The old fire station is at 701 13th Avenue South.

SOMEONE WATCHING OVER ME
Oliver's Lodge, Murrells Inlet, South Carolina

. . . .

This story began in South Carolina back in the 1940s—the back-of-the-bus days when everyone took segregation for granted and rest rooms had "colored" painted on one door and "white" on the other. Those who know South Carolina well say it is a state of contradictions, where emotions between races run high about a Confederate battle flag yet astonishing acts of kindness also occur.

The setting is Oliver's Lodge at Murrells Inlet. Diners sit gazing out the windows at colors like those of a melting Van Gogh painting. The late afternoon sun transforms the marsh grass into a sea of molten gold, then a glowing buff. As darkness sets in, the jet black crescent of Garden City across the water is strewn with lights.

Oliver's Lodge is a rustic, weathered place started nearly a century ago by a steamboat captain on the Waccamaw River. Leaving the river for good, Captain Bill Oliver and his wife, Emma, opened a fishing and hunting lodge at Murrells Inlet during the early 1900s. Then came their retirement, and Captain Bill's son, Mack, continued the business, but as a restaurant. Oliver's Lodge became one of the first coastal restaurants to serve local seafood, instead of the traditional southern fare of fried chicken and country ham. It was famous for its roast oysters, fresh fish of all kinds, soft-shell crabs, and delectable patties made from the carefully picked meat of the local hard-shell crabs.

Tourists heard of it, and for them, as well as the natives, dining here became a tradition. It was not uncommon to see out-of-state couples returning on the same date each year. The restaurant seems to draw people back.

During the 1940s, when Mack Oliver ran it, he would rise about six o'clock for breakfast and a short while later hear the padding of bare feet on the back porch. When he opened the kitchen door he would find several black boys holding buckets filled with live blue crabs, their claws waving desperately in the air. The boys had caught them at daybreak and were bringing them to the lodge to sell. The youngest of the group was an engaging seven year old whose given name was Roosevelt, but the others called him "Rooster."

Rooster would rise at dawn at his house in a community called Waccamaw Plantation, where he lived with eleven brothers and sisters. Then he would head off to meet his friends and catch crabs. In the first light the boys skittered here and there on the tidelands chasing the elusive creatures. With the swift jab of a forked stick they would pin the crab's claws down, scoop it up, and plop it into their bucket.

But one morning Rooster didn't join the other boys. The reason was his daddy, a daddy who was the cause of most of the trouble in Rooster's world. His father usually began drinking in the evening, and by dawn he was lying on the sofa passed out. When he woke up, Rooster didn't want to be there. That was the way it was that morning, so Rooster tried to dress very quietly and slip out of the house without being heard. But suddenly the snores on the sofa ceased, and his father opened his bloodshot eyes. His gaze fell upon the boy. Rooster tells the story of what happened, even to the words, although it was long ago.

"My father started by asking, 'Where's that kindlin' wood you s'posed to fetch, Rooster? I don't see it. That means you ain't brought it in, you sorry little rascal. I'll learn you.' On unsteady legs he rose from the sofa and stood in front of me. I tried to dodge past him, but he filled my path. His big hands grabbed me. Daddy slung me around, and, taking both my wrists, he secured them with his belt, then looped it over the wooden bar that held the door closed.

"Walking over to the wall where a pile of switches lay over two wooden pegs, he very deliberately picked out a limber one and brought the switch down across my back, then my legs. I felt it burning like a stingray out in the surf as it wound around and around me and I shouted, 'Daddy—stop, stop!'

My momma stood there crying and begging, 'Stop. Please stop, oh please!' over and over, but he never seemed to pay her any attention no matter how much she begged him.

"Finally Daddy decided he wanted some 'bacca out of his jacket on the back porch. He went after it, hollering back, 'Don't you be goin' nowhere, young 'un. I ain't through with you yet.' But I got that strap off my wrists and was out the door. When my feet hit the ground, they were flying.

"All I had on was my undershirt—no pants," he recalls.

"I ran past a white man I knew, and he called to me, 'Rooster, where's your pants, boy?'

" 'I got shorts on, sir,' I called back and kept running.

"I ran two miles, until I had no breath left when I reached Oliver's Lodge. All I could do was crawl into the cool darkness under the porch, my body and neck on fire from the pain of the switch."

Maxine, Mr. Oliver's daughter, says that later that morning when her father went down the steps, he heard a sound coming from somewhere nearby. A sound like a whimpering puppy. Getting down on his knees, his eyes probed the darkness beneath the porch until they rested on something white—Rooster's undershirt. The boy's face was turned toward him, and when he saw him, he called in a weak voice, "Mistuh Mack. Oh—oh, Mistuh Mack," and he crawled painfully out into the sunlight.

"Rooster! Who did this to you?" asked Mack Oliver, his blue eyes dark with rage. "Tell me!"

"My daddy."

Mack Oliver took him into the house, where his wife, Teeny, lifted the undershirt. Long red stripes curled savagely around the small body from his legs up to his neck. Teeny Oliver bathed the raw welts raised by the "limber switch" and spread salve on them; then, after they fed him, Mack Oliver told Rooster to get into the car. At first Rooster hesitated, afraid he was being taken home. "Don't worry, we're not going to your daddy's house," said Mr. Oliver quietly. "Just get in." They drove to Pawleys Island, where Mack Oliver knocked on the door of the magistrate's office.

"This is Roosevelt Pickett," he said to the magistrate. The name "Pickett" had come down from plantation days when slaves received the surname of their owners. Gently peeling back Rooster's shirt to expose the bloody stripes for the magistrate to see, Oliver said, "His father beat the pure tar out of him, and I'm not letting this child go home."

"What are you going to do with the boy, Mack?" asked the magistrate.

"Take care of him, that's what," came the reply.

The magistrate looked surprised, then shrugged. "Well, I'll try to help you all I can," he said. "But first I'm going to have to go over and talk with his father." Mr. Oliver and Rooster drove back to Murrells Inlet. Late that afternoon the magistrate's dusty, dark blue Plymouth sedan turned off Highway 17 into the narrow road to the lodge and parked near the giant live oak between the lodge and the marshlands.

"Mack, I went over there and told Roosevelt's father he hadn't oughta whip any kid the way he did Rooster, and I'd send him to jail if he did it again. I think I scared him up pretty good. 'Course he wants Rooster back but says he's willing to let him stay at your place 'til he wants to come home."

Rooster never went home, nor did he ever speak to his father again.

The Olivers' daughter, Maxine, was eleven then, and she and the little boy soon became fast friends. "I didn't think anything about Mom and Dad taking him in," Maxine says now with a shrug. "They just told me he needed help. Mother bought his clothes, and on Christmas morning he had presents just like the rest of us."

From the day Mack Oliver found Roosevelt curled up under the front porch, the Oliver family took care of him. They fed and clothed him, took him to the doctor when he needed to go, and saw that he attended school. Mack Oliver taught him how to cook, clean, and make house repairs. In his teens, when Rooster developed a rare eye disease, the Olivers took him to specialists at the College of Charleston, then Duke, and finally Emory, but the top medical schools had no cure. The doctors were unable to save his left eye.

That never stopped Rooster from doing his job at the lodge. "If hands and feet are needed to do it, I can get it done," he says today. He also kept his connection with his mother, taking part of his pay check to her every week as long as she lived.

"Mr. Oliver would get me up every morning about six o'clock, saying, 'Roosevelt, hit the deck.' I'd help him fix breakfast—earlier on Sunday because of church—but if it was a weekday, we'd eat together and then he would start me to cleaning or show me how to do some repair around the lodge. About seven-thirty, Mr. Hawkins, Maxine's husband, would come over. He would take about fifty or sixty pounds of food saved from the restaurant the night before, and sometimes we'd pick up more from the Animal Right to Life Organization, which he had founded.

"Then we would head out on our route. Each morning there must have been a hundred cats sitting beside Turntable Road waiting. There were also mother dogs with puppies. Sometimes we could get the animals adopted. Once I saw something move in a dumpster, and when I reached down and uncovered it, it was a tiny kitten! Jane and Mickey Spillane adopted that one."

It never seems to have occurred to Rooster that one day Mack Oliver, and even their daughter, Maxine, would not be able to run Oliver's Lodge any longer. That was unthinkable. They were his people, along with his own mother, whom he depended upon and who meant everything to him.

But the time came when they put the lodge up for sale. Rooster, a tall, calm man, whose present-day beard lends dignity to his expression, was unperturbed. While they waited for a buyer, he continued to catch crabs for the table, repair the pier and house, and stand in the dining room looking out through the windows at the fall hurricanes. One morning the Olivers called him into the kitchen where they had all worked together for many years and, with deep sadness, broke the news that the restaurant had been sold. "I thought that was the end for me at Oliver's Lodge," said Rooster.

But that would have been out of character for Mack Oliver. He made the sale contingent on Rooster's being given a free room in the lodge for life. Rooster began to perform similar duties for the new owners.

He liked to watch the storms. During the third week of September in 1989 he heard that a worse storm than usual was on the way. Everyone was calling it Hugo. Rooster knew that all of the tourists and most of the natives were evacuating. Maxine asked him to stay at her house with them, but he didn't think it was necessary. He never had left the lodge for a storm. That night he was awakened by the rain beating wildly on his windows. He sat on the edge of his bed looking out, lit a cigarette, and forgot to smoke it when something hurtled past his window. Going downstairs, he went over to the windows across the front of the lodge dining room to get a better view. He watched the wind tear the lodge pier off its pilings. He had fished there often. Still, he wasn't afraid.

The next morning he saw the ground covered with debris in every direction. Large boats had been plucked out of the water by the wind and hurled 200 yards or more across Highway 17. The entire second floor dining room of a well-known seafood restaurant nearby had been blown away, and he was shaken. For the first time Rooster realized how easily that gust of tornado-like wind could have struck just a mile south and sliced off part of Oliver's Lodge. He heard the weather report on the radio calling Hugo the worst storm in fifty years. The old lodge had weathered it and sheltered him once more.

The soft-spoken black man sums it up. "I guess it takes seeing something like Hurricane Hugo to start you thinking. I wouldn't have believed I would ever get away from Daddy. Then to be taken in by the Olivers and have them treat me like family. I think Someone has to be looking after me who really cares about my life—and maybe Mr. Oliver puts in a good word for me up there now and then."

· · · · · ·

Oliver's Lodge is on the water and cannot be seen from the road. The sign for it is beside the road at 4204 Business Highway 17, Murrells Inlet.

DOES THE GRAY MAN STILL WALK?
Pawleys Island, South Carolina

. . . .

Captain Nance's Restaurant at Murrells Inlet is one of my favorite seafood places, and when oysters are in season, I am irresistibly drawn there. One night in March of 1998 my husband and I had arrived later than usual, and although we were sitting at one of the coveted tables overlooking the water, the beautiful view had been lost in the gathering darkness. It was almost eight o'clock now, and lights across the water traced the curved arc of land that is Garden City.

After our waitperson took our order, my husband asked her, "Do you happen to know any ghost stories in this area?"

"I know about something that happened to me," she replied. She was a gray-haired, grandmotherly looking lady in her early sixties.

"Tell us about it," I said with interest.

"One morning I was driving back to Pawleys from my job at the paper mill in Georgetown. I knew I was driving too fast. When you've worked all night, you're tired—so tired you get careless."

We saw her customers at a nearby table signal her. She nodded to let them know she would be there, then glanced down at her Timex watch. "I'm sorry," she said. "You see how busy we are right now, but if you will wait until . . . say about eight-thirty, I'll be glad to tell you how it happened." There was a flash of something akin to fear in her blue eyes as she recalled it.

Wait? For what promised to be a good story? Of course we could. This is an area that is rich in ghost lore.

We began to speculate about what our waitperson would tell us. Every time I came to the South Carolina coast thinking I knew all of its secrets, I would hear something astounding. The Low Country stories seem inexhaustible, and I constantly hear new ones, not stories from a hundred years ago, but supernatural occurrences that are going on right now.

"Do you really believe that some man dressed in gray warns people on Pawleys Island before hurricanes?" my husband asked as we waited. When I first started writing, I found the story of the gray man the most difficult to believe. The tragedy that is said to be the origin of the story occurred about two hundred years ago.

Some believe that the gray man is Percival Pawley, who founded Pawleys Island, but I think yet another tale is more apt to be the true basis. Older residents of the island have said that the gray man is the ghost of a young man from a prominent family who died out on Pawleys in 1800. Returning from a long sea voyage, he was in high spirits. His wedding was to take place soon, and, along with a family servant, he was on his way, for the first time since his return, to visit his fiancée.

He was so eager to see the girl that he rode at a reckless pace, not heeding the warnings of his servant. His horse stumbled and threw him into a pocket of quicksand. There, despite his struggles, he was rapidly drawn beneath the surface of the wet sand! The spirit of the young lover who died such a horrible death is said to stay on to warn and protect others from disaster. Over the years many claim to have seen his ghost striding along the beach or in the vicinity of Pawleys. Descriptions never match. Some say he is a faceless apparition.

In one of my books the ghost of the gray man warned a family from Georgetown to leave the island. That was just two hours before Hurricane Hazel struck with no warning. In another story a young woman from Charleston was told to leave the island late at night while she was in the family beach house all alone! When the gray man visits a family before an approaching hurricane, he directs them to leave the island immediately. Oddly enough, when they return to their house, they are surprised to find nothing has been damaged. No sand has been deposited on the ground floor by receding water, no towels blown off the line where they had been carefully hung, no toys washed off the porch and left strewn about the beach.

My husband and I discussed what families have said after three different storms. All they can report is, "We were warned to leave immediately. We don't know who the man could have been. Only that he visited no other family on the island." They have never seen him before in their lives.

"Has TV ever done anything on it?" asked my husband.

"As it happens, I was one of the advisers for a TV episode produced by *Unsolved Mysteries* about the phenomenon. When it was filmed, three couples met in Georgetown to describe their encounters with the gray man."

Most of the customers were gone now, and as the last tables were being cleared, our waitperson, Joyce, joined us for coffee and began the story she had promised us.

"It was one morning when I was leaving work at Georgetown to come home to Pawleys. It was late September, and I will never forget what a scare it gave me. When I walked out of the paper mill after work that morning, I remember thinking how tired I was and that I didn't feel like making the drive back home to the island. It wasn't even eight o'clock in the morning, and I already knew it would be a sweltering day. I could hardly wait to take a shower and go to sleep in my air-conditioned bedroom.

"I walked over to my dark blue Chrysler—you remember all that chrome they used to have—that's what it looked like. Sliding behind the wheel, I headed north in the direction of Pawleys Island. Up ahead the sky was full of dark, chunky clouds like a bad storm was coming. I looked at my gas gauge. I could probably make it, and I wanted to get home and to bed. Then I recall seeing a convenience store and thinking to myself, I really should go ahead and fill up the tank. It delayed me a little, but I comforted myself with a honey bun for the road and drove on.

"When I was almost to Pawleys, the clouds had grown more ominous, and a fine rain began to fall. I was sleepy, and I noticed myself repeatedly drifting over the line in the middle of the road. Then I turned the wheel back too quickly to straighten the car, and it skidded. Without my realizing it, my Reebok was pressing down harder on the accelerator than I thought. I tried to be more alert and drove on three or four more miles. Then it happened again, and that really woke me up, but by now I was almost at the island. It's crazy to drive when you are this tired, I thought, and began thinking for the umpteenth time about getting a job nearer Pawleys Island that would pay as well as the one I had in Georgetown.

"Darn! I was winging it down the road again. Clouds of mist went flying past my side windows, and suddenly, for a terrifying moment, the road ahead was completely blotted out. Then there was an instant of heartfelt relief when it cleared, but, as I zoomed around a curve at about seventy miles an hour, I saw a man standing squarely in my path.

"There was no time to think, only to furiously pump the brakes, and I did. Surely the crazy fellow would move, but he didn't. He just stood there in the morning mist, wearing some sort of old-timey clothes with his arms spread out like a cornfield scarecrow. I was almost upon him. I stomped down so hard on that brake pedal that I thought my foot would go clean through the floor. I knew that would throw the Chrysler into a nasty skid, and it did. My tires screeched like banshees and I began sliding all over the wet asphalt. How I straightened the car out and stopped, I will never know.

"When I peered through the windshield, there he was, still standing right in front of me, but as I sat gaping at him he suddenly disappeared!

"Edging the car forward a foot or two, I stared out searching the shoulders on both sides of the road for a figure. Not a soul could be seen. As the sun burned through the mist ahead, I remember groaning weakly, 'O-o-oh!' and then breaking out in a cold perspiration. I felt faint, for I had narrowly escaped my worst nightmare.

"In the middle of my lane just a few feet ahead of me was a flatbed truck that had dropped a load of pine trees—the biggest trees I had ever seen. They had broken loose from the chains holding them on the truck and rested on the asphalt right in my path! Fixed to the end of the last log someone had tied a red bandanna. I got out of my car, and walked toward the cab of the truck to speak to the driver. It was empty. Nor was anyone to be seen along the shoulders.

"I have always had a horror of being behind one of these flatbeds and having its load slip the chains. I could visualize the giant-size burden falling either in front of me or off the side of the truck on top of me as I passed. Barreling along at the speed I was going, if I had not seen the man standing there and managed to stop, I would have collided with the logs piled up like jackstraws and been killed.

"And then I thought, if I hadn't taken those few more minutes to stop and fill up with gas before I left Georgetown for Pawleys, I might have been traveling right behind it when those logs dropped."

My husband looked at her with awe. "Joyce, was that the famous gray man warning you?"

"All I know is I saw that man standing right in the middle of the lane in front of me," she replied, "and whoever he was . . . he was God's doing."

In my years of writing, I have heard many variants of this well-known South Carolina story. Accounts of the gray man, as seen by different people, may be found in two of my other books, *Ghosts of the Carolinas* and *South Carolina Ghosts from the Coast to the Mountains*.

THE LEGENDARY HUGO
McClellanville, South Carolina

● ●

George Metts's desk calendar read Thursday, September 21, 1989. He had known for several days that Hurricane Hugo would probably strike the South Carolina coast that night. Metts was an experienced paramedic who had been on duty through many a hurricane, but he knew that this time, with all the storm warnings, most homeowners had left the area to go inland.

"Of course, there would always be a few diehards who would stay," he thought. "They would be inside their waterfront houses now, waiting out the storm. He visualized them laughing and joking as people did at hurricane parties, watching TV reports, rising from their game of penny-ante poker to pour themselves another drink or frowning with concentration over how to bid their bridge hand. Later some of the guests would fall asleep on a sofa or guest room bed while others took their place in the game.

"The roar of the wind and rat-tat-tat of the rain pelting the house gave these events just the right taste of danger, making an exciting backdrop for the sociability within." He remembered the young couple in the jeep riding along the beach that afternoon, probably loving the excitement of it, heads turned seaward to feel the spray in their face from the charging breakers.

Warnings that this storm could be dangerous had come well in advance, and more people than usual had headed inland, some to Columbia and even a few to Charlotte.

In some ways Metts was probably much like other men. He was married, loved his wife and three children—a girl and two boys—and sometimes worked long hours. But it was his job that was different. You could never predict when something was going to happen, and from the moment a call came in to Medic Six Station he was under intense pressure. He might be speeding to the scene to help an accident or crime victim, transporting someone to the hospital, or giving assistance at any type of disaster. Paramedics can be compared to the lifesaving crews of the Carolina coast before the present-day coast guard stations were built. Courage, a willingness to face personal danger, and swift judgment are necessary qualities. Like the early lifesavers who went out time after time into a boiling surf, Metts was a born rescuer.

His assignment came Thursday evening to go to the shelter at Lincoln High School in McClellanville, and he was confident that he could meet any challenges that lay ahead. Expecting long hours of grueling work and bone-weariness later, he had no premonition of a greater personal danger than usual. It was fortunate that he was a man who dealt calmly with whatever happened.

Metts and a good friend of his, fellow medic Tim Lockridge, drenched by gusts of wind and squalls of rain, carried their equipment and supplies into the arts-and-crafts room. They arranged their boxes of medical supplies brought from the station, and since there was nothing else to do, they hung up their wet clothes to dry and used the craft tables as makeshift bunks. They talked now and then but mostly attended to the job at hand. Metts and Tim could anticipate what was needed, and they made a good team. An hour later a man stuck his head in the door and asked, "Can you bring an invalid over here from my house?"

He led them there in the blackest night imaginable, no streetlights or house lights. They found the invalid and his frightened wife waiting in the house. By flashlight Metts and Tim brought the man out on a stretcher, packed his wheelchair into their unit, and rushed the man and his wife to the school. The rain was now so hard it stung their cheeks. Minutes later someone else ducked his head in the door. "Can you go and pick up my Uncle Joe?" he asked. Metts had already gone by Joe's late that afternoon, and the man had refused to come to the shelter. He shook his head and said, "Sorry. The winds are too high now. He will probably be OK."

*Miraculous stories
have been told by some
Carolinians who survived
the devastation wrought
by Hurricane Hugo.
(Photograph courtesy of
the Village Museum,
McClellanville, South
Carolina)*

Now the storm was at its peak, and in the cafeteria not far from them the lights had gone out. Tim was attempting to read, and Metts lay on the table unable to sleep. The lights in their room went out, and except for the hall emergency lights, the entire school was plunged into darkness. Then the hall lights were gone too. There was nothing to do now until the storm was over, so they both tried to rest and succeeded in dozing off to sleep.

"Then . . . I don't know how it happened," says Metts, "but somehow, in my sleep, I heard a voice say, 'Get up!'

"Startled wide awake in seconds, I was struck by a silence so total it was eerie. I sensed rather than knew that something was terribly wrong. Then I heard it. It was the swooshing sound of rushing water very near us. I waked Tim, and as I hurriedly shoved my feet into my shoes to go and find the source, I glanced over at the baseboard air-conditioners. They were swelling in toward us, and water surged and gurgled between the vents.

"We ran back and forth piling valuable equipment on the table as the water rose around our feet. It was soon ankle deep, and I abandoned any attempt to place personal gear where it would stay dry. Together Tim and I managed to wrench open the door into the hall so that we could get out. I felt the water rising higher around my legs. As we reached the cafeteria, the door unexpectedly came open in my hand and pulled me through it in seconds, but the rapidly rising water inside slammed the door shut behind me.

"I tried to pull it open, staring helplessly at Tim's horrified face pressed against the glass of the door. He pushed back, but to no avail. He was trapped, and with a sick feeling, I knew it. I was on one side with the parents and children we were to help, and my partner was shut out in the hall, the door held closed by the water within the cafeteria. Tim and I were now out of contact with each other; our dispatcher and our walkie-talkies were out of commission. There was nothing I could do for him.

"On my side of the door the cafeteria was full of people, and everyone was rushing toward the stage. If the people in that room were to survive, it was my duty to help them.

"I waded over to the wall and began to lift women and children up on a table. Everyone looked frightened, but they were still keeping very quiet. Of course, there was always the danger that panic would spread through the crowd. Children were already crying, and a few women on the stage were hysterical, but fortunately their hysteria had not yet spread. The people near them took control, calming them.

"Out in the hall, Jennings Austin, the principal of Lincoln High, dashed past the glass doors of the cafeteria, a screaming crowd following behind him as he sought some exit—any exit—from the building. A few minutes later he passed going in the opposite direction, his frantic entourage following close behind him. Regardless of what exit the principal tried, the doors were all held closed by the force of the water coming in from the ocean. I looked through the glass in the door at them, my eyes searching the crowd. Where was Tim?

"I could see out through the tall plexiglass windows and the water out there was higher than the water on our side of the glass, which was up to my waist. Someone took a fire extinguisher and began banging it against the windows but stopped when people began shouting, 'No! No!' They realized that if the water from outside came in, it would raise the level in the room and we would all drown.

"'Our Father who art in heaven . . .' Desperately I began to pray the

Lord's Prayer. 'Hallowed be thy name,' and then my mind went blank. As many times as I have said it, I couldn't remember the rest!

"A black lady stood near me with two small children, and I asked, 'May I hold the young one there for you?' In minutes the water had risen to my chest. She handed me the three-year-old, whose name was Tsara. I tried to comfort the little girl by talking and singing. Then I attempted to quiet a hysterical woman who, afraid that she would fall beneath the water, began to hyperventilate. The water was growing deeper by the second, and I knew that if she fell she would take others down with her.

"Several people appeared agitated already by her calls for help. Somehow I had to calm her down, so I spoke as quietly as I could to her so others would stay cool. I was every bit as frightened as everybody else but knew I had to hang on to myself. In the midst of these thoughts I thought of Tim and hoped he had found a table or something high to stand on.

"Now the water was up over my chest, and I could smell cooking grease and gasoline fumes from cars. That meant that the water must be deep enough for stoves and cars to be floating around outside the school. I kept saying, 'Please, Lord, don't let me drop this kid,' at the same time praying for my own little girl and family. Were they in a safe place? I talked to the child, continuing to hold her above water level. On the other side of the room someone had gotten up on the roof and broken a top window pane. A few had climbed to safety, but I knew the women couldn't swim across the cafeteria, nor could I, not holding a three year old.

"I watched the clock on the wall. What accurate time it kept, but the hands seem to move so slowly! What was I doing to help anybody? My job is to be a paramedic, I thought. Am I letting people down? Then I realized that I was just as helpless as anyone else. All of us could drown right here in one mass grave.

"When we realized the water had finally stopped rising, there was a great sense of relief. It was about five o'clock in the morning that I gave the child back to her mother and watched them walk out with everyone else. The life-threatening experience had lasted only about two or three hours, but if the water had stayed that high much longer, some would have drowned and others would have suffered hypothermia.

"The first person I saw outside was Tim, and we stopped to give each other a bear hug. He had been up on the roof hanging on for dear life in that wind!

"An off-duty constable and I searched the school for bodies in the knee-high water. I remember being thankful that we didn't find any. Outside, houses had been swept off their foundations and out into the middle of the road. Water was bubbling up here and there like a witch's brew. I knew it might be coming from gas mains, and that's scary. Parts of Business Highway 17 were completely washed away. Everywhere there was this unnatural quiet, no people, no traffic, not even any chirping of birds; nor did the birds begin to sing again until midmorning.

"I didn't realize until later that a seventeen-foot wall of water called a 'storm surge' had struck the school. Lincoln High, designated as a shelter, was about ten feet above sea level, not the twenty feet the hurricane evacuation study had estimated.

"I think that with more than eleven hundred people trapped in that school, it was the protecting hand of God that none of us died," says the medic wonderingly. For George Metts, these recollections will always be just beneath the surface of his mind. "I do what I have to do when storms come, but even now, if the wind begins blowing really hard, memories of Hugo come flooding back. Then I feel the hairs on the back of my neck rise."

Hurricane Hugo hit the Carolinas more than a decade ago. It is said to have been the worst storm in fifty years. Soon afterward people wore shirts boasting, "I Survived Hugo" to show that even after the unthinkable had happened they were still here. In the areas hardest hit, it is still the storm against which all other storms are measured.

. . . .

For more than a century, when ships headed out of Charleston Harbor, they passed over the heads of nine dead men. The men lay restlessly tossing and shifting on the bottom of the sea in the confinement of their metal coffin, the *H. L. Hunley*, a Confederate submarine. They waited for the world of the living to resurrect their remains and honor their bravery. One man has played a significant role in the drama of the *Hunley*. He is Dr. E. Lee Spence.

Spence began his underwater history and treasure hunting in 1960, when he was only twelve. "It's a wonder I didn't kill myself during those early years," he admits with a boyish grin. He made his own diving gear from a fire extinguisher canister. By the standards of what he would use in later years his equipment was primitive, but his research was professional and his luck monumental.

The tall blond diver and marine archaeologist went on to discover some of the world's most famous shipwrecks and write articles for prestigious journals describing his discoveries and the artifacts brought up. His finds of hitherto undiscovered and amazingly intact shipwrecks attracted the praise and interest of numerous individuals and institutions, including Captain Jacques Cousteau, director of the Institut Oceanographique, *National Geographic* magazine, the National Park Service, and the director of the Underwater Exploration Program of the Smithsonian.

Since his early teens the young diver had a dream. Most divers hope to find a Spanish galleon laden with gold, but Lee Spence's dream of a lifetime was to find the *H. L. Hunley*. Discovering history is what excited him most, and somewhere at the bottom of Charleston Harbor lay the Confederate submarine long recognized as the greatest naval innovation in over two thousand years.

Lee Spence had listened with fascination as men speculated about its possible location. He had researched accounts of the trial runs of the *Hunley*, of its mechanical workings, and of its crew. As a professional diver, he well knew the perils of underwater exploration.

This is the story Dr. E. Lee Spence reconstructs of the *Hunley* mission.

"During the most dangerous months of the Civil War, while the city of Charleston was shelled almost daily by the Union blockade, the *Hunley* made ready for action. It was just after twilight on the evening of February 17, 1864, that nine men, dressed in new Confederate uniforms, two of them sporting the gold braid of officers, walked eagerly to Breach Inlet near Charleston. They hurried so as not to be caught and stranded by the ebbing tide.

"As the last of the nine man-crew squeezed into place along the submarine's heavy crankshaft, the hatches were dogged shut. Sweat began to break out upon the men's brows, and they resisted the first stirrings of claustrophobia—then panic. They bravely managed to thrust both emotions aside. Gears screeched with a metallic sound as the men forced the crank around and around until they were just beyond the harbor. Here and there in the metal interior of the sub their eyes watched drops of moisture slide down the walls.

"Of course what the bold and colorful George Trenholm, chief of sixty Confederate blockade runners, hoped, along with General Beauregard, was that a submarine attack would not only sink one of the powerful Union blockaders, gathered like hawks in the harbor, but disrupt the entire Federal blockade of Charleston.

"On that crisp, cold February night in 1864 three gleaming lanterns in a row pointed seaward from the Confederate Battery Marshall at the eastern end of Sullivan's Island. Meantime, just offshore on the ebbing tide, Lieutenant Dixon and his crew edged slowly through the mirrorlike sea. The long, lethal body of the submarine headed west toward the Union blockade, its destination the channel off Morris Island. Here the pride of the

Dr. E. Lee Spence comes up from a dive.
(Photograph by Nancy Butler)

Union navy, the new warship *Housatonic*, lay at anchor. Unsuspected by its crew, the ship was in mortal danger.

"Ballasted to float with her hatch just above the water, the *Hunley* made a difficult target at night, but at this moment every man was tense. They were passing a Union picket boat. Would they be seen? Lieutenant Dixon held his breath. A spy had warned the Union navy that the Confederates might launch some unknown underwater weapon. But their pickets did not seem to notice the submarine; and so its black, cigarlike body wallowed furtively past them in the dark.

"Peering out the tiny dead light in the submarine's forward hatch, Dixon tried not to think about some of the disastrous earlier experiments with this craft. He had heard stories of the contorted faces of the dead crew, described by men who had had the sad task of dismembering and pulling the stiffened bodies from the salvaged submarine. He went over in his mind whether those sinkings were just bad luck or errors that could have been avoided.

"Fingering the lucky gold coin from his fiancée in his pocket, he repeated to himself that the heavily dented coin had once saved his life from a bullet. Would it bring him luck again? Dixon had not accepted this command believing that he and his men would face certain death. Granted the tiny sub was not easy to maneuver, but he and his crew had taken the boat out nightly on drills and they had always returned. All that was different tonight was that this was no practice. Now they were approaching their target.

"The submarine was barely big enough to accommodate nine men, who were able to turn the crankshaft in such a confined space only by contorting their bodies and turning the crank over and over in unison. Lieutenant Dixon scanned the faces of his crew and, seeing their exhaustion, called for a few minutes rest from the effort.

"The candle in the submarine flickered erratically, showing a lack of oxygen, and some of the men were beginning to grow nauseated. Dixon immediately raised the breathing tubes so that a slight breeze struck the men's cheeks, freshening the air. This lifted their spirits, and their mission now seemed possible.

"They were not far from the *Housatonic*, where they planned to embed their torpedo, placing it below the waterline in the hull of the huge Union blockader. Then they would back off a suitable distance and detonate the charge. Their torpedo contained ninety pounds of gunpowder and was fastened to the end of a twenty-foot spar on the bow of their craft. The barb of the torpedo would hold it mortally embedded in the hull of the *Housatonic* while they backed away. At a safe distance they would pull the lanyard and detonate the torpedo.

"But what was a safe distance, thought Lieutenant Dixon, and as a precaution he unbolted the hatches and threw them open. They would at least provide an escape route if the sub sank.

"The faces of the men on the submarine were grim and detached as they approached the Union blockader and Lieutenant Dixon was finally able see the large bold letters forming the name *Housatonic* on her side. Then, looming up before his tiny sub, was the immense, heavily armed ship, her decks filled with patrolling sailors. Suddenly one of the lookouts halted and stared straight down at the submarine.

The lookout had almost decided that what he saw was a floating log when he realized "the log" had changed course and was moving diagonally across the flow of water. It was the secret weapon the blockaders had been told to watch for! He shouted the alarm, raised his musket, and fired several times in the direction of the submarine, but he was too late. There was a roar like a clap of thunder and a bright flash that set the sky on fire. On the other vessels men saw the sailors run to abandon ship as the *Housatonic*, reeling from the torpedo's blow, began to sink. Within three minutes she was beneath the water.

And what happened to the *Hunley*? It is believed that the submarine survived the initial blast but, finding herself in the midst of the rescue operations, unwisely chose to submerge. Whether a deadlight or seam blew out is unknown, but water pouring into the submarine blocked the men's escape. Divers came out and dragged around the wrecked blockader but failed ever to find the submarine."

Although E. Lee Spence had spent many hours searching for the *Hunley* with sophisticated electronic equipment, that is not what he was doing in November of 1970. He was on a trip to fish for sea bass. Traps had been set off the *Miss Inah*, captained by Joe Porcell, and two of the traps had hung up off the stern. Spence, diving to retrieve them, followed the fish traps down to the bottom and peered through the gloom. It was only previous research he had done that caused him to notice the strange appearance of a dark, rusted ledge upon which one of the traps was caught.

Landing almost on top of a narrow cylindrical object that formed a long ledge in the sand, he broke off a slender yellow sea whip that protruded from it and carefully rubbed the spot on which it had grown. When he withdrew his finger, he saw the greasy black smudge made from years of rust. Then his eyes traced the outline of the almost cylindrical shape that tapered off into the sand. At the end nearest him he noticed the raised marks of hand-hammered rivets. He thought of all the days spent in libraries— studying notes, diagrams, maps, and charts, reading through endless rolls of microfilm—and knew he had found the *Hunley*.

"The dream was beneath my fingers. I wanted to stay down there and savor it forever," says E. Lee Spence; "but on the other hand, I wanted to share it immediately!"

Filled with excitement, and a certain lack of caution, Spence shot up to the surface, shouting to the men in the boat, "I've found it! I've found the Hunley!"

It is not so surprising that a man of Dr. Spence's experience should make this dramatic discovery and produce the necessary maps to confirm it. What is amazing is that for 105 years divers searched in vain for the wreck of the world's first submarine to sink a warship. In fact, after the event in 1864, it would be fifty years before any other submarine would duplicate this feat. In 1970 Spence became the first person to report the location of this historic weapon of warfare to the state of South Carolina.

Later, at the official request of the *Hunley* Commission, Spence donated his rights to the submarine to the state of South Carolina. The value of the *Hunley* is estimated at over $25 million. Someday, South Carolinian Dr. E. Lee Spence will receive formal recognition for his discovery in both the annals of naval warfare and the history of his native state.

After its restoration, the *H. L. Hunley* will be on display at the Charleston Museum of History, 360 Meeting St. (843-722-2996).

THE MYSTERY AT FORT SUMTER
Charleston, South Carolina

· ·

No one knew better than Major Robert Anderson that he was sitting on a shell that could explode at any moment. On December 20, 1860, the secessionist convention in Charleston notified Washington that the state had seceded from the Union. As far as the state authorities were concerned, South Carolina was now an independent nation. The continued presence of a Union fort in Charleston Harbor inflamed Confederates, who had sent repeated requests to Washington, through southern sympathizers, to negotiate a peaceful withdrawal of Fort Sumter's Union troops. When these requests were ignored, the Confederate reaction was predictable—force.

Trapped here with no promise of military reinforcements to come to his aid, Major Anderson was as unhappy as the southerners who surrounded him. He too had sent countless messages to Washington—appeals to President Lincoln warning him of the potentially explosive situation. The messages asking Lincoln to recognize the seriousness of the situation and act were ignored by the new and inexperienced president. Major Anderson requested that the president either supply Fort Sumter with reinforcements or grant him permission to withdraw. Lincoln did neither.

The fort did not have enough men to repulse the strong Confederate attack that Anderson knew would come, and he would be forced to defend the flimsy wooden barracks of an unfinished fort against a heavy assault. Even Fort Sumter's own powder magazine was a danger, apt to explode under enemy bombardment.

By early April, more requests reached Anderson from the Confederates, asking him to withdraw peacefully to avoid bloodshed. Daily the major hoped to receive orders from Washington to leave the fort, but none arrived. In the late afternoon of April 11, 1860, Major Anderson sat at his desk writing another report. He knew now that the Confederates would probably launch their attack that night. He rose from his desk and asked his adjutant to summon Captain Foster.

"See that the men sleep in the bomb shelters tonight. Have they made an area safe for the wounded?"

"Yes sir."

"What about the ammunition?"

"It's been distributed to the guns, sir."

"Have the men enlarge the storage area. Captain Gustavus Fox is going to attempt to land with supplies."

"Attempt, sir?" repeated the officer. Then he reddened. "Sorry, sir."

"If he's got any chance to get through, it will be tonight," said Anderson, lips pressed tight and face drawn.

"Yes, sir. We will watch for Officer Fox, sir, and we're doing everything possible to seal the rest of the fort. I have men filling sandbags and piling them up on the parapet. That may protect us against the rebel guns from Sullivan's Island."

He gave the major a quick salute and hurried back to supervise the men, who resembled ants as they carried their bulky loads to and fro in the wan light of a new moon. They labored until ten o'clock that night. Foster himself watched and listened for naval officer Gustavus Fox to approach the fort with tugboats bearing supplies for the Union troops.

Just after midnight the Confederates delivered a last ultimatum to Anderson. It was a promise not to fire if the Union troops would evacuate peacefully. Then they waited several hours for a reply. Finally it came. Major Anderson said he would evacuate in about three days—but only if he didn't receive supplies and became hungry. This reply did not elicit a good response from General Beauregard.

Without waiting for the three days to pass, or for the major to get hungry, the angry Confederates fired a shell to signal the beginning of the bombardment. Anderson, who had gone to bed, waked to a scene that might have been straight from his worst nightmare. A floating ironclad battery was anchored off Sullivan's Island with the barrels of its guns firing at his left flank, and as he watched, Confederate soldiers streamed out of their boats to occupy every island surrounding Fort Sumter.

The unfortunate Major Anderson had written increasingly blunt warnings to inform President Lincoln of the threat to the Union fort. He had waited for replies to them but received none. Now the Confederates were attacking his men. His guns on Fort Sumter could blast the Confederates out of the water, and that was exactly what he wanted to do, but unless he heard from Lincoln he had no authority even to defend himself. The major watched the battle in helpless frustration.

Thirty-four hours later, with the wooden barracks and officers' quarters in flames, Anderson was forced to surrender. Miraculously no one had been killed, but a strange incident took place. In surrendering, Anderson requested that when his garrison left the fort the following afternoon he be allowed to give a 100-gun salute to his tattered Union flag before lowering it. The Confederates granted his request. When the forty-seventh round of the salute was fired, the cartridge in Union private Daniel Hough's gun exploded as he was driving it down the barrel. The explosion blew his right arm from his shoulder, mortally wounding him, and sparks touched off other cartridges that lay nearby.

That same afternoon, while the evacuation was going on, Private Daniel Hough's own company buried him, presenting arms as the body was lowered into the soft, sandy soil of Fort Sumter. A naval chaplain from the city read a prayer. Next morning, just before finishing their last night's tour of duty inside the fort, three of the Union soldiers fashioned a wooden headboard for Hough's grave.

More than a century later, in the late 1990s, Arnold Ashby, a visitor from Kentucky, was at the fort touring the museum when he thought he experienced the breath of another person upon the back of his neck. Moving slightly to to one side, he glimpsed a puff of gray smoke in the air above him. He could have sworn that there was the acrid scent of gunpowder in the air. Turning, he was shocked to see what he took to be the blue-coated form of a soldier. For a matter of seconds Ashby glimpsed a face with a moustache, beard, and well-defined nose.

These were his only impressions as the man melted into the crowd of tourists pressing to view the exhibits. Only the scent of gunpowder, lingered and Ashby found himself feeling sick. When had he last smelled powder like that? he asked himself, and the answer was at a reenactment.

After that first battle of the Civil War, a strange thing happened to the flag that had flown over the fort. To the immediate right of the center star, the flag faded and left a white spot. In that lighter area the outline of a man's face became imprinted. The man was Private Daniel Hough. He was wearing a Union cap, and beneath it his features were visible—closed eyes, mustache, nose, and beard. The flag is displayed in a glass case in the Fort Sumter Museum. Others, like this writer, believe that the image of Private Hough's face on the flag is most clearly visible in the third white stripe just to the left of the black vertical line.

Hough's ghost is said still to inhabit the fort and his apparition is seen most often in mid-April.

Four years to the day after Anderson surrendered Fort Sumter, on April 14, 1865, he returned for a ceremony of celebration to mark the fort's return to Union hands. The ceremony was made more jubilant by receipt of the news that General Robert E. Lee had surrendered his army. At the stroke of noon on April 14, 1865, General Robert Anderson raised his garrison flag over Fort Sumter again. President Lincoln did not attend the ceremony. He and his wife had a previous engagement at Ford's Theater in Washington, D.C. He would not appear at Fort Sumter or anywhere else ever again, for that night President Lincoln was assassinated.

· · · · · ·

Tours going out to Fort Sumter leave the Charleston waterfront several times a day. For hours, phone 843-722-169.

HAG-RIDDEN ALMOST TO DEATH
Mount Pleasant, South Carolina

. . . .

The slim black woman slid with catlike grace into the chair opposite me at the restaurant. Heads turned, and the diners at nearby tables observed her smart black and tan silk dress, her hair swept back from her face, in a large, smooth chignon. Her manner was all business, but the Gullah story Kenya Barnes began to tell me in her velvety soft voice made me shiver. It had nothing to do with the New South.

"I was raised in a big old two-story white house in Awendaw, a farming town about twenty miles up the road from Charleston. Growing up there as a child, we all believed in ghosts . . . some still do. We didn't call these particular kind of spirits ghosts. They were worse than that . . . they were hags. I knew two people in that little town who everyone knew were hags. It was a man and a woman. But let me tell you about the man. He was the worst . . . big, with a build like Santa Claus, but he didn't look or act like Santa. That man—he was evil." I listened to Kenya spellbound.

"Back then nobody stayed shut up in their houses. Everybody went to visit everybody else . . . we all knew each other. The big, evil man would visit too, but his visits weren't like those of the rest. They were different. That night after everyone else had left your house and you went to bed, he would come back and even if you hid under the covers, he would return as a hag and find you. After the house had been silent for a while, you could feel him there. Then he was on you and it was awful. I know just what it was like because it happened to me.

"He rode me. Oh, how he rode me! I couldn't breathe and I thought I was smothering. I remember trying to move a toe or a finger but couldn't.

I felt numb. I waited, wanting to tear myself away from him, but I couldn't move until he let me up. What they always do is come back the next day to see if you are all right. That is one way you know them. Sure enough, he came back the next day to see.

"We had a way to find out if this man really was a hag. I'm going to call him, 'Mr. Tom,' because his real name is still known in that little town. I don't want to say that name even to you.

"When he came to visit, someone would slip into another room and put the end of a needle into a match flame. Then one of us would go out and stick the needle into one of those big footprints of his out in the yard. If he was a true 'hag' he couldn't leave until the needle was removed, but, because he was a hag, he knew the needle was out there. Finally, someone would go out and remove it; then he would go along home and not bother you for a long, long time. He knew that you knew what he was about.

"If 'Mr. Tom' was going to visit you, he prepared himself first. He would strike a match and put it to the tip of his finger until it burned the end off his fingernail, and after he did that burning, starting with that finger, he would peel the skin back until he peeled himself right out of his skin. Now he was ready to slip into your room in the middle of the night. I know what it was like, for it happened to me as a girl. The hag had been to visit us, and, sure enough, the next day he came walking up through our front yard. He had returned.

"I remember looking up at him and saying, 'Mr. Tom, are you a hag? Did you ride me last night?' I remember that large, heavy body turning slowly around toward me and that ugly face of his looking down so angry.

"'Oh, great God!' he exclaimed. 'This child has no manners. She must have gotten that from the old people.' Furious, he turned and left.

"If you ever thought a hag was going to visit you, there were ways to protect yourself. Of course, you could stuff a rag in the keyhole, but one of the best ways is to toss some salt outside your door. Then the last thing before you go to bed at night you take more salt and you sprinkle it all around your bed. Don't you miss an inch!

"I promise you, no one without skin is going to want to feel the sting of that salt on them. Now those are methods all of us knew, and I remember them to this very day. Watch out or it can happen to you. You will wake up in the morning exhausted as if someone has been trying to smother you in the night. You can't half breathe. You feel numb—unable to move.

"Don't ever let anyone tell you that being hag-ridden by someone is just old people's talk or a superstition. It's not—it's horrible and it's true!"

THE GRAY HOST NEAR EDISTO
Ashepoo, South Carolina

· ·

There are still a few very old men who remember hearing the one-time slaves on Edisto Island talk of Civil War days. The slaves listened avidly to former soldiers who had served in the Federal ranks, and they heard the southern side from friends who were Confederate body servants. Some of the slaves continued to serve the young planters they had grown up with who fought for the Confederacy. But by the 1930s only a handful of former slaves were left who recalled the stirring days when they heard "the big guns shoot." For them nothing would ever match the 1860s.

Sometimes soldiers fought in the fields the slaves had just cultivated, skirmished along the very roads they had walked that day, or—Yankee or Rebel—died a few feet from their cabins. Old William Rose, who lived down at Seaside on Edisto, was a mere youth during the war, but, having had some schooling, he talked well. In later years Rose could occasionally be persuaded to tell one of his stories about "Rebel times." Although he used "modified Gullah," he was perfectly understandable and his speech had the richness of Afro-English words mingled with the rhythmic flow of Gullah.

One February day in the 1930s a reporter named C. S. Murray was interviewing him for the *Charleston News and Courier* when William Rose began to philosophize about bravery in warfare, both ancient and modern.

"Men don't know what they fight for," Rose said. "They think they fight for some fine, shining thing, but who knows." Then he began to talk of the effect war has on people, and he told a story.

"The bravest thing I ever saw was at Ashepoo Junction on the Charleston & Savannah Railroad. Train loads of Confederate troops passed through there on their way to the battlefields. It was nearing the end of the war. Grant was ready to smack Richmond, and Sherman was marching tromp, tromp, tromp across Georgia. I was just a young lad then, and I had to see and hear it all. One day the plantation overseer sent me to Ashepoo Junction to get the mail." The old man's eyes sparkled, and he was like a little boy again, reliving one of the most exciting moments of his life.

"That afternoon, when I reached Ashepoo, the train was just rolling in. Smoke from the engine was in the air everywhere, and car after car was filled with Confederates. They come shouting in from Charleston bound for the upcountry. Seem like I got there just in time to see what was going on.

"I stood near the long trestle and watched the train rock by. One engine was in the front pulling; one was in the back pushing, pushing, pushing. The train was loaded down with soldiers. They thick as peas. They ridin' all over the car roof. They shout and holler. I was much amazed to see such a lot of soldiers—all going down to die.

"And as they go across the trestle over the river, they start to sing. One pick a banjo, one play the fiddle. They sing and whoop, they laugh; 'Good-bye,' they holler out to the people around the train, 'Good-bye!' All of them are going down to die.

"And it seems to me that is the most wonderful sight I ever saw. All those soldiers, laughing lightly, singing and shouting that way, and all of them going down to die. One soldier shouted, 'Well boys, we're going to cut the Yankee throat. We are going to meet him, and he better tremble because we are on our way. Our gun is greased and our bayonet sharp. Boys, we are going to eat our dinner in hell tonight.'

"One gang riding on top of a car was playing cards. I saw them hold up a card, plain as day, when their luck was right. They were going to face battle, and yet they play cards and sing and laugh like they were in their own house . . . all going down to die. The train pulled across the trestle. I stood up and watched the men until the last car pulled out of sight. The last thing I heard was the soldiers songs. . . . All going down to die.

"When I got home I went to some of the old people. I said, 'How can a man act like that?' and they answer me: 'That ain't nothing. They used to it.' But I still wonder and wonder to this day; how can those soldiers laugh and sing and talk about 'dinner in hell' when they going down to die?"

"Ashepoo is still here, between Jacksonboro and Green Pond, not far from Highway 17," says John Jeffries, who lives there. "It's just a wide place in the road now. All we have is two filling stations and the manufacturing plant. Let me tell you an experience I had here.

"It was a cold February night in the 1960s when the dark came down fast and there was no moon. I had worked late at the plant and was walking home along Main Street not far from the railroad tracks when I began to hear a sound way off down the tracks growing louder and louder.

"It was a long, plaintive train whistle, followed by the sound in the distance of men singing, but the voices were not clear enough for me to hear all the words well. I caught fragments of them 'Hurrah! Hurrah!' and 'the bonnie blue flag forever' echoed through the stillness of the night. Now I'm a southerner, and I knew that tune, for it was one my mother had played many years ago on the piano . . . a Civil War song. I heard the long hiss from a steam locomotive and, strangest of all, for maybe half a minute—the ring of men's laughter."

Then all was quiet. Jeffries said he stood there wondering. Where could the train be and the men who had been singing? And where had that long drawn-out eerie whistle come from through the cold night air? As far as he could see, nothing was there now—just a railroad track in a little town slam dunk in the middle of nowhere. Puzzled, he shook his head. Was it the ghosts of long-dead Confederate troops going through Ashepoo on their way north?

A NIGHT TO REMEMBER
John Cross Tavern, Beaufort, South Carolina

. . . .

The village of Beaufort was a buccaneer haven in 1718, and the John Cross Tavern a place for pirates to relax and brag about their prizes—stolen cargoes of tea, spices, silk, and rum. They were snug as could be, their ships anchored in some virtually hidden inlet among the sixty-eight islands off the South Carolina coast.

Now and then in the tavern one of the pirates snapped a bit off the stem of his clay pipe and, raising it to his lips, inhaled the tobacco deeply, then swigged from his bottle of rum as he sang a coarse song. Another, with a sweeping drunken toast to his lady, might overturn an oil lamp. Someone would grab for it wildly, replace it, and start a song. With a wink at the women they clasped, the men clanked their pewter mugs spiritedly on the bar to punctuate a phrase of their song. Scarves held back their head locks, and many wore pistols under their belts or cutlasses at their sides.

"You're pretty as ever I saw you, Anne," shouted tall, handsome Captain Sam Bellamy to Jack Rackham's companion, Anne Bonny. The jealous Rackham, his face flushing with anger, reached for his knife.

"Sheath it, Jack!" called out beautiful red-haired Anne Bonny contemptuously, "or Sam will have your liver!"

Two or three of Rackham's crew closed in around him and dissuaded him from a fight that might have ended disastrously at the hands of a better man. Evenings seldom went by without some near-violent incident or boisterous play. Anne Bonny sat in the tavern at one of the small tables near the wall and smiled as she, like the men, bit off the end of one of the clay pipes, a nod to sanitation. She provocatively returned Captain Bellamy's wink.

"Back to the ship with you, my girl," shouted Rackham angrily. She paid no heed to him, and began to walk toward Bellamy. As she passed, Captain Edward Low reached out and clasped her bare arm with his hand.

"Get your dirty paw off me, Eddie," she cried, turning with sudden fury and knocking his hand away. "Watch yourself, Anne!" warned Rackham. Edward Low had an explosive temper. He also had a cruel streak, and few of the pirates in the room wished to cross him. The angry curses of Low followed Anne and Rackham as she rejoined him and the pair left the tavern.

These were the days when you looked sharp if you put out to sea from Beaufort Harbor. Pirates might lurk behind any of the many islands, ready to pounce. In the days when former sea captain John Cross opened his tavern and lodging house, two thousand buccaneers roamed the Atlantic coast. There was Captain Edward Teach, better known as "Blackbeard"; Captain Sam Bellamy, well known around Provincetown, Massachusetts, who sailed the *Whydah*, after the African city of that name; Captain Edward Low from London, whose ship was ironically dubbed *The Happy Delivery*; Captain Billy Lewis, who sailed the *Morning Star* and captured ships off the Carolina coast until 1726. And then there was "Calico Jack" Rackham and his beautiful red-haired sweetheart, Anne Bonny. Dangerous cutthroats and sea robbers all, from New England they sailed the length of the American coast and on to distant waters like the Red Sea, busy with commerce between Europe and Asia, coming home to sell their stolen cargo at Charleston, Baltimore, Philadelphia, New York, and Boston.

In the 1700s, places along the coast like the John Cross Tavern were few and far between. There a respectable man could drink hot grog and find decent lodging, but he sometimes found himself mingling with the pirates who also patronized the tavern. John Wesley, a founder of the Methodist faith, found lodging at the John Cross Tavern August 3, 1736, on his way to England.

Today voices are raised and glasses ring at the tavern just as they did almost three hundred years ago. This early two-story building, strong because its walls are built of a mixture of lime and oyster shells called "tabby," still stands on Beaufort's Bay Street. Both restaurant and tavern are now

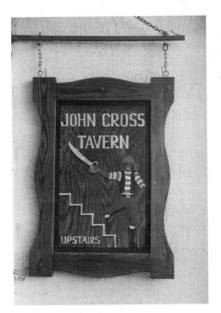

This wooden sign directs visitors to the John Cross Tavern. The owner of the tavern says there were signs of a ghost from the day he opened.

upstairs. Those who would stop for a meal must watch for the colorful picture of a pirate on the ground floor at the left side of the building. An arrow beside it indicates the outside stairs by which patrons mount to the second floor. When owner Harry Chakides restored the John Cross Tavern to its original use, he found four floors had been placed one on top of the other in the course of its history. The tavern room has the original molding, similar to some in Williamsburg, Virginia.

For the past four decades Citadel graduate Chakides has looked out over the Beaufort River and the docks where barks and brigantines, with sails billowing in the breeze, once lay at anchor. Beaufort once vied with Charleston for the honor of being the most popular South Carolina port, as the town has a fine natural harbor. Unfortunately, however, it is indefensible.

"Some of the spirits of the tavern's early past are still here," says Chakides. "I knew it the first week. Mother and I were cleaning, and she was in the other room. I heard her say, 'All right now, come out and let me see you!' I called to her saying, 'What's the matter, Mother?'"

"'One of those chairs just started moving back and forth,' she replied. 'It must be the ghost, so I challenged it to show itself.'"

There were two more strange incidents the first week Harry opened. "I had a girl cleaning on the second floor, and she came tumbling down the stairs in a panic, crying, 'Someone up there is calling my name!'

"I said, 'Oh, it's just the ghost. Don't worry. He's friendly.' She calmed down.

"Another incident occurred regarding some heavy boxes we had moved in and arranged along the hall to unpack. When I looked for them and didn't see them at first, someone started laughing, and I said, 'Are you laughing at me?' 'No,' he said. 'Look. Someone has moved all our packing boxes to the other side of the hall!'

"But the most eerie happening was one night when I had stayed here all alone to clean the large room downstairs. It was late, and I swept and scrubbed and polished, humming as I worked. Little by little, I became aware of soft, rustling, persistent noises. I was sure I heard footsteps on the floor above, then voices mingled with the sound of tussling, and I flew up the stairs.

"All along one wall shadows were moving—the shadows of human beings. Amazed, I began to try the finger games I had done as a child to see if I could reproduce shadows that looked like people but none of my finger play changed one movement on that wall. The shadows continued to gesture and gyrate, moving independently of me. I have never discovered the cause.

"But the ghost is different. Its presence is often felt here near the entrance to the dining room. It is where a partition between two rooms was taken out to make one larger one. I have been told that in this case the person who lived in one of those rooms may return as a ghost but not understand what has happened to the room he once had. Perhaps that is the case with the place near the entrance to the dining room. It is here that the spot of chillingly cold air is felt."

Years ago salesmen going to a town would live for a while in a lodging house like this while they did business locally. Sometimes they might stay several months, and occasionally they died (of what we hope were natural causes) in these rooms. Several present-day guests have mentioned feeling a chill in certain rooms.

Others believe they have experienced a cold sepulchral hand resting on their shoulder! I like to think that the touch is a concerned one from the spirit of John Wesley returning to implore someone to repent. Or perhaps it is the hand of tavernkeeper John Cross himself, calming a rowdy customer. Although some believe they have been seized by the viselike fingers of pirate captain Edward Low trying to shanghai them out the back door to his ship!

But what really happens late at night in this old building? Are shadow images of pirates with gross and terrifying faces moving across the wall of the tavern tonight? Do the spirits of Blackbeard, Edward Low, Billy Lewis, Anne Bonny and "Calico Jack" Rackham ever return from "the bad place," and does their return ever crisscross with that of present-day guests at night in the John Cross Tavern?

· · · · · ·

The John Cross Tavern, located at 812 Bay Street, is open for breakfast, lunch, and dinner (phone 843-524-3993).

THE ADMIRAL'S WIFE
Anchorage House, Beaufort, South Carolina

. . . .

Everyone who has ever discovered this unique coastal town knows that at some point on the highway entering Beaufort you have gone back in time. You have entered a world where one street after another is lined with magnificent Revolutionary and Civil War period homes. As if to confirm this, you will see an old cemetery in which lie citizens who have passed on before the rest of us—those who defended this land from Indians, skirmished with pirates, battled the British, and reluctantly hosted the Union army. Does a town like Beaufort have ghosts? Of course it does.

In addition to the house called "the Castle" and the old John Cross Tavern, we must place another name on the list of local sites that have apparitions. "The Anchorage has been known to be haunted for years," according to Fredree Kedge, former owner. This enormous white house, with its Corinthian columns, is one of the most impressive overlooking the bay. Mrs. Kedge and her late husband owned and operated it as a bed and breakfast.

The lady describes herself as an agnostic but says: "Whatever inhabits that house is an entity that showed up the first Thanksgiving after we opened it. People would complain, saying 'Someone bumped me as I was coming down the stairs,' or 'There were areas we walked through where we noticed a considerable chill.'"

Of course Mrs. Kedge began to search her mind for the possible presence of people who had lived here who might have an attachment to the house. The first was William Elliott's family. Mr. Elliott built this house just before the Revolution. Then there was the pre–Civil War William El-

Anchorage House has had the reputation of being haunted for years. Just ask the marines who have been frightened when they worked there.

liott III. A maverick, he opposed secession and resigned his seat in the South Carolina Senate rather than vote for nullification. On the other hand, he was violently pro-southern and in favor of slavery, probably because he owned twelve plantations and could ill afford to lose his laborers. With these views he managed to anger both his southern and northern friends.

But Elliott remained a staunch Unionist until war broke out, and then, like Robert E. Lee, he went along with his state. During the occupation of Beaufort, his house was turned into a hospital, like many other homes in town. One of its claims to fame is that in 1876 Wade Hampton, a former Confederate general who had actually freed his own slaves before the Civil War, made a speech to the citizens of Beaufort from the front porch during his campaign for governor.

Thus far we have several possible situations for ghostly activities, but Mrs. Kedge has long thought that, of those who have lived here, the ghost most likely to haunt the Anchorage is that of the admiral's wife. In the early 1900s retired naval officer Admiral Beardsley purchased the William Elliott House, and he and his wife spent $80,000 remodeling it. Of course, everyone knows how admirals are, and it is said that Mrs. Beardsley was also a person of strong opinions. In any case, she must have cared deeply about the admiral, for she kept his ashes on the mantel for many years after his demise. In time, the Anchorage became a guest house.

When visitors asked where "the entity" was, Mrs. Kedge told them, "Anywhere it is damp and cold." It was most often sensed as coming from the lower level—an updraft of air that came blasting upstairs. Mrs. Kedge says, "We had the air-conditioning system redone, but no sooner had we finished than in the lounge there were complaints that now the cold air was worse than ever. When there were large dinners served, the Anchorage would hire extra help, Mrs. Kedge usually hiring several marines from the nearby base at Parris Island. They too became aware of the "entity."

According to a lady who worked at the Anchorage for many years, the basement is the place where things happen, and some servants are reluctant to go down there. The most startling experience was that of a marine from the base. Working at the inn for the evening, this young man entered the cellar to bring up a famed merlot for a banquet. When he reached for a bottle of it, he found himself at a standoff with a fierce-looking figure swathed in bandages who was holding an upraised sword! "The marine fled up the stairs from the basement screaming!" says Mrs. Kedge.

Others have been equally terrified. Whether they experienced an unexplained blast of cold air, met the ghost of the admiral's wife, or saw apparitions from Civil War days when the Anchorage was a hospital, is unknown. But it must take quite an awe-inspiring apparition to shake the nerves of a marine.

．．．．．．

The Anchorage is not open to the public at this time. It is located at 1102 Bay Street.

Hilton Head Island, South Carolina

. . . .

O ld ruins and old legends live side by side beneath the moss-draped live oaks that grace Hilton Head Island, and if something supernatural happens here, visitors to this picturesque island should not find such an occurrence surprising. This is the story of a strange phenomenon out of the past being repeated in the present.

Have you ever wondered what happens to old ghosts? I have often asked myself whether the apparitions people have seen that I wrote about in my earlier books still appear. A letter I received recently from a Hilton Head visitor may provide an answer.

As background let me summarize the story of Martin Baynard and Victoria Stoney from my book *South Carolina Ghosts from the Coast to the Mountains*.

Marriages in the Old South were sometimes for love and sometimes arranged by the families because of large property holdings. Both seem to have been the case at Hilton Head when John and Elizabeth Stoney announced the engagement of their only daughter, Victoria Ann, to Martin Baynard. The wedding was to take place in August some years before the Civil War.

In the meantime, each afternoon the pair would ride in Martin's cabriolet down winding sandy roads lined with pines and scrub oaks. Occasionally they would stop if either saw something interesting. "Isn't that an old slave graveyard over there among the trees?" Victoria asked on one of these rides. When they got out and went over to look at a small mound of freshly dug earth, Victoria was touched. "It's the grave of a little girl," she said "and here is her doll." She picked the doll up from the grave, studied it curiously, and put it back beside the small cup and spoon nearby. Then she lifted the cup.

"Put that down!" said Martin, more sharply than he had intended, for he was disturbed without knowing why. She replaced the cup on the grave.

"The Gullahs have different beliefs from our own," he warned her.

But who could have told them that danger lay not in some Gullah superstition but rather in contagion from a deadly fever that would strike Victoria down.

A few days later the shining carriage which was to have carried the young pair away was draped not with celebratory white ribbons but with the black ribbons of death. Much to everyone's astonishment, in the midst of his sweetheart's funeral Martin's carriage dashed madly out of the cemetery. It was only a matter of hours before he himself died from the fever.

On the very night of the day his body was placed in the family mausoleum there were strange reports of his apparition driving the carriage. Some said they heard the thunder of horses' hooves, while others felt a rush of cold air as a carriage sped past. A few were sure they had seen an impressive gold-and-black carriage racing beside the foaming surf or hurtling along down island roads in the moonlight. Viewers always mentioned the fluttering black ribbons streaming in the wind.

But if you are really interested in whether there could be any truth to these old stories, look over my shoulder and share with me the following letter I received recently from a lady who vacations each August on Hilton Head. Then judge her experience for yourself. Here is what she says:

My husband mentioned, when he managed to contact you by phone, that I wanted to relate an incident I experienced last summer at Hilton Head Island. It is now a year later, and after reading your book *South Carolina Ghosts from the Coast to the Mountains* for the first time, I was immediately struck by the similarity of a story of yours with my experience last summer.

We have been staying at Hilton Head Island since the summer of 1984, and nothing like this had ever happened to me before. It was August of 1996. There was going to be a full moon on the last Wednesday night of the month, and I knew it would be lovely.

Late the night of the 28th it became cloudy, and I grew more disappointed by the moment as I sat alone waiting to see the moon rise over the water. Everyone else had gone to bed, and I sat by myself on the upper deck of our villa. Suddenly I had the bold idea of going down to the beach alone. The surf was unusually rough that night due to Hurricane Edward out at sea. I thought to myself that if I were out there on the beach I could revel in the sight of that moon full above the water. I still had hopes that it would suddenly appear, and if it did, this would be a night to remember.

High tide had occurred approximately at 9:05 P.M. I looked at my watch, and the time was now midnight. Should I go inside to find a flashlight? It seemed unimportant, so I started off without it. When I reached the end of the narrow wooden walkway and was about to step down into the sand, my peripheral vision caught an enormous speeding shadow at my right. My heart began to pound wildly.

All was quiet save for the sound of the surf. Then I felt a sudden rush of wind strike my body, and the shadow rolled past. It seemed to touch and meet the fingers of foam at the edge of the surf. Up the beach it stopped. To my utter amazement the tall dark form of a man got out of the carriage and stood beside it staring back in my direction. I cannot describe the energy that I felt emanating from him. I have never felt so afraid, so utterly vulnerable and alone.

Turning around, I dashed recklessly back over the wooden walkway, through the grass, and up the steps of our villa, with no desire to look back. As I tried to unlock the patio door, my hands trembled and my fingers moved awkwardly. Should I go out through the door upstairs and try to catch another glimpse of what I had just seen from the upper deck? Was it still there? I didn't have the courage to find out! I stood inside my bedroom with my back against the door trying to catch my breath. Then I ran to the windows and doors, locking them hastily, turned off all the lights, and got into bed. I went over that scene in my mind, tossing sleeplessly until daybreak.

Next morning I hurried out and searched for signs of a carriage, or any marks whatsoever on the sand. I don't know just what I hoped to find, but whatever I had seen left no traces. I am not convinced that my family really believed me when I related my experience, but, on the other hand, there is no doubt at all in my mind about what I had seen that night. I found it strange and foreboding.

This summer we all returned to Hilton Head for our annual family visit together the last week of August. Nothing out of the ordinary took place, but I did discover your book in Author's Store at the Village at Wexford. There it lay in the store window, and my daughter and I both saw it at the same moment. I bought it on that day, which was Thursday the 28th, the anniversary of the date I had seen the carriage the year before.

Perhaps the death of Martin Baynard's fiancée occurred on the same date in August that the dark carriage came hurtling toward me beside the water? Had Martin Baynard and the Stoney family once lived in the area where we stay—or if it was characteristic of him to rage at fate and express his grief with such abandon—I would surely have the answer to the strange sight of that night—the specter of a man who had been dead for two hundred years! Was he accompanied by his once-beautiful bride? I shivered.

As I opened your book and for the first time read the story, *There Goes Martin Baynard's Carriage*, I was chilled to the bone. Every hair on the back of my neck stood up. His carriage is what I must have seen on the beach that night and I am filled with awe."

Shirley Sigmon
September 11, 1997

If you are at Hilton Head during the latter part of August, stroll the beach at the midnight hour. You may see a black funeral carriage hurtling along near the foaming surf—or feel the wind as it rushes past.

III

Georgia

OLDE HARBOUR INN
East Factors Walk, Savannah, Georgia

. . . .

R uss Mitchell knew a great deal about Savannah, for it was one of the places his wife traveled on business. They had often stayed there when he was in the military on leave because they both loved Savannah's beauty and its good restaurants. Mitchell is a tall, distinguished-looking man with graying hair. He has a military bearing, exudes confidence, and gives the impression of being very much in control. And so he is. His talent is solving daily management problems.

When he became general manager of the elegant Olde Harbour Inn on River Street, the last thing he had any interest in was Savannah's reputation for ghosts. In fact, if the conversation took a turn in that direction, he was usually quick to say, "All nothing but superstition."

The Old Harbour Inn was built in 1892, on the bluff overlooking harbor activity. Since so much of Savannah revolves around the water and ships, it is not surprising that the enormous ceiling beams in the suites were salvaged from old sailing ships. If these beams could talk, they could tell tales of storms, hurricanes, mutinies, piracy, and other exciting events at sea.

The impressive leaded-glass doors of the inn's main entrance face River Street off East Factors Walk. The wide, dark floor boards, the oriental rugs, the high ceilings, and the late Victorian decor all contribute to the inn's atmosphere of quiet luxury and comfort.

Present-day guests enter unaware of what once went on in this place. From the walls echoed the shouts of slaves unloading ships' cargoes, the creaking of huge wooden hoists, the clatter of oaken casks of rum striking the planks of the dock. All of this took place amidst the calls of well-dressed factors, who had left their offices above the warehouses and come out-doors to buy and sell, mingled with the Gullah and tribal languages of the African Americans. The slaves joked with each other, exchanged news, or sang as they unloaded the cargo and carried it into the warehouses along the waterfront.

Russ Mitchell had tried to give his wife a picture of what riverside life was once like, both at ground level and along the Factors Walk. At the top of the bluff, on the level of the city street, the walk was now lined with small shops, a steady stream of curious tourists wandering from one to another.

"In those early days here it was very different," says Mitchell. "From ship, to dock, to the damp basements of the warehouses, black slaves glis-tening with sweat hoisted bound boxes of cargo and even bales of cotton from the first floor up through holes in the second floor. Just imagine this river as the life blood of Savannah's commerce and, from the early years until the Civil War, cotton as the city's gleaming white flesh. Cotton brought the wealth that built the magnificent homes around our beautiful city squares. That along with the money of a Civil War blockade runner who used his millions to help rebuild the impoverished city.

"When was the Harbour Inn building built?" his wife asked.

"Sometime in the 1890s. Like most of the buildings below the bluff, this was built as a warehouse, not an inn."

"And the part with our suite?"

"The East End, or early part of this building, was built about 1907, be-fore the fire. It was about that time that the legend of a man called 'Hank' began. From the time I came here, I heard the old stories about Hank. Someone mentioned him first at a 1995 sales meeting."

"What kind of stories were they?" she asked.

"Crazy stuff. He worked here during the early 1900s. They say he was a troublemaker from the beginning. Nothing suited him. The factors pro-vided his living quarters in this building, and he was always complaining about them or the people he worked with.

"Did he give any serious trouble?" his wife asked.

"Everyone suspected that he was the one who set the old warehouse

fire. His anger must have done him in, for he was the only person who died in the fire. Let's forget him. I've never thought it was worth talking about."

They both enjoyed exploring the riverside shops, and then they went up to their suite at the inn. His wife, who had just returned from a business trip, was tired and fell asleep almost immediately. Russ sat up reading but was in bed before midnight. He had fallen asleep when he heard his wife calling him. This is how he tells it:

"Sound asleep, I dimly heard my wife's voice saying, 'Russ! Russ! Wake up!'

"She shook me. 'Someone is trying to get into our room.' It took a minute or so to penetrate, but I got up, walked sleepily over and opened the door to the hall. No one was there and it was two-thirty in the morning.

"The first thing I thought of was the stories about Hank, and that made me realize how superstitious we can be without realizing it. The hall was completely empty, so I closed the door and got back in bed. I was almost asleep when I heard a noise. The handle of the door was turning. This was too much! I went back and opened it again. Nothing!

"I stationed myself very quietly behind it and stared out through the peephole into the hall. As I stood there the door handle only few inches away from my waist began to turn. My heart began going a mile a minute. I snatched that door open ready for whoever—but the hall was empty.

"'Come in, Hank,' I said loudly. Nothing stirred. I stayed awake watching the door handle for quite a while but that was the last time it turned that night.

"The next morning my wife sat on the bed putting on her pumps when suddenly she jumped up, face white. 'Russ, someone is sitting on this bed with me!'

"I could see no one, but she was sure someone was there."

Is Hank the restless spirit at the Olde Harbour Inn? No one knows, but the guests write surprising notes and leave them for the staff. One guest wrote that he was sitting in a nonsmoking room when he sniffed the aroma of a strong cigar, and another guest reported that he returned to his suite to discover his luggage in a most extraordinary place—the bathroom tub!

Mr. Mitchell, the perfect example of a courteous, dignified former military man, tries to explain the Olde Harbour Inn ghost.

"It all seems to happen in what we call the East End, but I assure you Hank is an infrequent visitor."

· · · · · ·

The Olde Harbour Inn at 508 East Factors Walk has single rooms and lovely two bedroom suites overlooking the Savannah River. The suites are ideal for a family vacation. For the chance of an even more memorable trip, you might wish to reserve one of the rooms where the ghost has appeared. For information, phone 912-234-4100.

· ·

"**B**rute" Bailey turned off Bay Street at Drayton, swaggered down Drayton for a block, and stood looking through narrowed eyes at the bar on the opposite corner. The year was 1864, and Bailey had arrived in Savannah a week earlier, primed and ready for a good fight. Not a street fight, mind you, but an event at a stable or pub that would pay him a handsome sum—a fight with excited onlookers gambling and the opportunity to place bets himself with wealthy gentlemen.

Opening the door of the pub, he was greeted by the murmur of voices and that familiar yeasty fragrance of ale permeating the air. He felt at home, for it was much like many pubs he had visited in London. Now early evening, men had come by after work and were already at the tables eating and drinking. At the bar there was only a seat or two left. Bailey sat down beside a broad-shouldered, curly-haired young fellow who nodded in a friendly fashion and introduced himself. "Name's Jack O'Dwyer," he said, "And yours?"

"Bud Bailey, but they call me, 'Brute.'"

"'Brute.' And why would they call you that?" asked O'Dwyer curiously.

"Oh, it was during one of my fights that I got that handle."

"You're a Brit, aren't you?" said Jack.

"That's right."

"Do much fighting?"

Bailey countered with, "A little. How about you? Ever do any bare-knuckle fighting?" Bare-knuckle fighting was a bloody, dangerous sport later to be outlawed in England.

"A few times. Some of the gentlemen who watched said I was pretty good. They liked to bet on my fights at the stable. But I quit that a year ago. It ain't my cup o' tea now that I'm married to Maureen and we have a little one."

"How much money you making at the stable?"

When Jack O'Dwyer told him, Bailey threw back his head, with its mis-shapen ears, and chuckled in amusement.

"Why Jack, just one fight would put twenty times that amount in your pocket, and pile your cap high with bills too," he said. "But you probably don't need big bucks."

"Need it, what with havin' to take my wife to the doctor all the time? She ain't been herself since the baby come." He drained his glass. "Sure and begorra, I could use money all right."

"Two glasses of ale over here, my pretty miss," said Bailey to the barmaid.

"Well, Maureen might see it my way with business bad as it is, but who would I fight?" the Irishman mused under his breath, but Bailey overheard.

"Jack, I'm taking a liking to you, and I think I might be able to help you earn real money," said Bud Bailey with a wink at Jack and a clap on his back. "Now how about a match between you and me? That would give the blokes in this town some entertainment, wouldn't it?"

"Who would set it up?" asked Jack.

"You've met just the man to do that, too," said Bailey. "Well, what do you say, my friend? Is it a deal?" Jack nodded gratefully and stretched out his hand. The two shook. The manager of the pub had been listening in-tently from behind the bar.

He chimed in. "Why not have it right here, Jack?—in the back room, where everybody can see it."

"That's right," seconded a friend of his. "Our Jack's a tremendous good fighter. I saw him last year over at his stable."

The next day Jack began getting back in shape, aiming his blows at a bag of feed and skipping rope daily. He knew he had better train because he had seen Bailey throwing some punches, and he looked pretty good. Jack had not mentioned the upcoming fight to Maureen, but she was beginning to ask questions.

Churchill's Pub is a lively, friendly place despite the grisly shadow that some have seen on the wall.

"Tell me, Jack, what's keepin' you so late at the stable?" she asked.

"Just breakin' in a new horse," said Jack. "I've a gentleman who will pay me well for it."

Meanwhile the manager of the pub was taking bets on the upcoming fight, and Jack was amazed by the amounts that he heard many wealthy young men were betting. What he didn't like were reports that Bailey was telling everyone about all the fights he had won in England, and that if he went back, he would get a shot at the current British champion. When Jack asked Bailey what all this talk about his being a champion boxer back in England was, Bailey just grinned and said, "Don't worry, friend, I'm just trying to stir up interest. I'm an unknown here and you're the favorite. The purse is going to be $10,000 — $9,000 to the winner and $1,000 to the loser. That will probably be me."

For the first time Jack felt some doubts about his new friend. When he went home that night, Maureen said, "I hear my Jack's gettin' ready to fight some English boxin' champ? Everyone's talking about it." He tried to explain, but she wouldn't listen. "You don't know nothin' about what kind of man he is, Jack. I don't like him callin' himself 'Brute.'"

He was on the defensive, and he got angry. "You know there's no business at the stable with so many gentlemen off in the war, Maureen. What am I to do to take care of you and the baby?"

All she would do was to shake her head and say, "You should listen to what the good Father McGuire said when I talked to him after confession today, and that was 'Wait on the Lord.' He will help us."

"Maureen, we can't wait any longer. You need to go back to the doctor."

In November of 1864, on the afternoon of the fight, the manager of the pub pushed the tables and chairs against the walls of the back room. In the middle of the floor one of the men drew a chalk line called "scratch." If an opponent was too battered to "come up to scratch," the decision was awarded to the other fighter. If one boxer killed another, and it was not accidental, the boxer was disqualified. With no more in the way of rules than that, the two men were ready.

A cheer went up for Jack from the onlookers who knew and liked him. He was confident his fighting experience at the stable would see him through a bare-knuckle saloon fight. He was sure his youth and strength would tell, while Brute, although he had a small reach advantage, was older. The two men stood in the center of the room, each in the defensive position for bare-knuckle fighting—arms crossed and held out in front of his body to ward off blows.

Jack immediately took the offensive, while his friends called out encouragement. Brute blocked the blows with his forearms and seemed on the defensive, and Jack pummeled away at him, trying to land blows to the stomach while Brute didn't really have a go at him. After a few rounds of this, the crowd was jeering Brute. But it was soon evident that the Brit had considerable experience, and by the time they had fought ten three-minute rounds, Jack was growing tired.

Now Brute moved in and caught Jack under the chin with a right uppercut. Then, as Jack staggered slightly, Brute struck him a blow to the left temple that could easily crack a man's skull. The watching men groaned and surged in around the two fighters. The saloonkeeper shouted, "Get back! Get back!" and they moved away from the two fighters. Jack lay on the floor, stunned by the blow, but he managed to get up to scratch by the count of ten. His knuckles were bleeding copiously. Now he jigged around the floor, making furious head feints at Brute in an attempt to gain time to recover himself.

Brute was not fooled. His roundhouse swing caught Jack O'Dwyer on the cheek, and Jack fell to the floor again. In an instant, Brute was on top of him. He jabbed Jack's lower ribs hard with his knee. As the bell rang, he seized a handful of O'Dwyer's hair and held him while he began to pummel his face with his other hand. The bell continued to ring, but Brute Bailey's blows went on like those of a madman. When spectators pulled him off the young Irishman, Brute was shouting, "I win!, I win!"

Jack's friends shouted encouragement and tried to revive him. The crowd pressed forward for a better look at the young fighter, who lay on the floor without moving. A doctor pushed through the crowd, bathed the blood off Jack O'Dwyer's face, and looked at the eyes staring expressionless at the ceiling. "This man's dead," he said. There was a furious outcry from the Georgians. "Murderer, murderer!" they shouted. Seizing the Britisher, they forced a noose around his neck and threw the other end of the rope over an exposed beam of the high-ceilinged back room, despite Bailey's struggles and frightened screams for mercy.

"Mercy? Did you show any?" they shouted back. "You'll get the same mercy you gave our Jack. That's what you'll get."

About the time the noose had done its work, the crowd within heard the sharp clip-clop of horses' hooves cantering over the cobblestones outside. They heard loud shouts—"Sherman is coming!"—and the pub emptied rapidly. Those who were left behind hurriedly buried Brute Bailey in a shallow grave in the cellar and sent word to Jack O'Dwyer's family that his body would be brought home late that night. At a time like this the authorities had little interest in what was happening at the pub, but it was best to be cautious.

Not long afterward, talk began to circulate. Some of the tavern regulars said that the sound of a man's cries could sometimes be heard from the cellar—that the shadowy figure of a hanged man had been seen swinging to and fro late at night in the back room. And the story goes that to this day Churchill's Pub is haunted by the ghost of the man who murdered the young Irishman.

The gentleman who today conducts Savannah's Haunted Pub Tour says, "By the time the fight was over that day, everyone was either leaving Savannah or busy trying to hide whatever valuables they had, for word had spread that Sherman was entering the city. Savannah surrendered politely and began to do business with the enemy." That night, true to what the good Father McGuire had predicted to Jack's wife, there were so many horses in the city of Savannah that the stables had more horses to take care of than they had stalls for! And since the officers of the victorious Union army were filled with both ale and exuberance, their tips were generous indeed.

In recent years remodeling has changed the interior of the front room of the old building at the corner of Drayton and Bay Streets. A new pub, originally built in England and moved to Savannah, arrived in 1920, complete with everything an authentic English pub should have. In front of its gleaming bar stretches a smooth alabaster rail trimmed with brass, and the pub walls are covered with an impressive dark wood. But the back room looks much as it did more than a century ago. In the course of remodeling a building, strange discoveries are sometimes made. During the excavating necessary to install the new pub, workers uncovered a man's skeleton buried below the ground floor in a shallow grave. According to the coroner, the bones were those of a man who had been thirty to forty years old when he died. His death was estimated as having occurred in the 1860s. The cause—a broken neck.

If you are sitting in Churchill's back room enjoying a glass of Guinness stout some night, select a table under the high ceiling beam and watch attentively. You may glimpse the shadow of a hanged man swinging back and forth, back and forth, silhouetted against the wall!

· · · · · ·

Churchill's Pub, at 9 Drayton Street, is a popular, convivial place. It was featured in the book *Midnight in the Garden of Good and Evil*.

RAMBUNCTIOUS GHOSTS
Hamilton-Turner Inn, Savannah, Georgia

. . . .

It was a fine autumn afternoon in Savannah, and on the third floor of the French Empire mansion on Lafayette Square, Lillian gazed at her image in the gilt-framed mirror. I'm not a little girl anymore, she thought with approval.

"Papa, it's time for me to have a ball at night to celebrate my birthday," she announced at dinner.

"We shall consider it," said William Pugh Hamilton. "That is if your birthday doesn't come at an inconvenient time, of course, such as the night your mother and I are entertaining the ambassador. When is it, my dear?"

"Papa! You don't remember? Last year my party had to be postponed, and some of the guests weren't even notified in time. They appeared at the front door with their gifts, and I was dreadfully embarrassed." She flushed at the memory.

"Of course, my dear. We all were." Her father turned his head and looked at his daughter with some irritation.

"Just don't let your birthday come at a bad time this year, Lillian," said her brother, Frank, mockingly.

"Sometimes I think that not even my own family appreciates how hard I work for this city," complained their father.

Tears welled up suddenly in Lillian's large brown eyes. "Well, why can't you ever do anything with us?"

"I intend to. I have plans that I haven't even told you about. We are all going to spend a weekend over at Tybee Island. Another outing your mother and I have been discussing is a family picnic beside the river. Wouldn't that be nice?"

"If we ever do it," said William, speaking up for the first time. "I wonder you have time to think about us at all, Papa. You're so busy being president of the bank and the electric company and trying to get a railroad over to Tybee."

"Son, those are the things a man is remembered for—lasting services to his community. Now didn't I buy that nice pool table upstairs just so that all of you would have something to do when your mother and I were entertaining?"

"You certainly did, Papa. In fact we play so much that Lillian's the only girl I know who could take on a pool shark from the docks and beat him hands down," said Harvey.

"That's disgusting, Harvey!" replied his father. "Lillian, I will go check the date and let you know."

A few minutes later their father was back.

"What about my birthday on April 30, Papa?"

"I'm afraid the date of your birthday happens to fall on the night of our dinner party for an influential guest from Washington, but we will make it up to you my dear." Mr. Hamilton started back toward the hall. Lillian flung herself facedown and began to sob on the sumptuous red velvet chaise lounge.

"Be careful, my dear, you may get spots on that lounge," said her father, attempting to put his arms around her. She tore herself away, crying all the louder, and Mr. Hamilton retreated from the room. Frank's face flushed with anger and, staring after his father, he made a feigning motion with his arm as if to throw a pool ball at his father's back. "I'm going to show him someday, wait and see," Frank vowed.

"Even after he promises, he will be busy at the jewelry store, or he and Momma will be throwing another party for some bigwig," said William. "Then he forgets us." They looked over at their sister sympathetically.

Lillian was really the only one who could tell their father off and get away with it. Now she wiped her eyes and said to Frank, "You're going to show him—how? I heard Papa's own sister, Aunt Emily, say to Momma, 'The only time Samuel's face lights up is when he's talking about his electric company,' and Momma blushed!"

The Hamilton-Turner Inn has beauty, history—and perhaps a ghost who enjoys playing pool. (Photograph courtesy of the Hamilton-Turner Inn)

Hearing gleeful cries coming from their parents downstairs, the children moved to the top of the stairs to listen.

"Grover Cleveland's been elected. Hurrah! Hurrah . . . Hurrah!" they heard their father shout exuberantly, their mother joining him with little murmurs of excitement.

"I gave generously to his campaign, Sarah, and you can bet he won't forget that. Can't you just see us dancing at the inaugural ball? But we have an ambassador to entertain at our own ball in the spring. We must start on the guest list soon. There is lots of planning for you to do, and, Sarah, be sure to invite the most important people in town!"

It has been a long, long time since the Hamilton children frolicked upstairs on the third floor of the old house. And it was close to a century later when an attractive blonde lady stood staring at the towering gray mansion. Later to be known as "Mandy" in John Berendt's book *Midnight in the Garden of Good and Evil*, the lady's name was Nancy Hillis. She had known immediately that of all the beautiful houses she had seen in Savannah, this was the one for her. She visualized herself entertaining here—guests crowding about the piano as she played and sang for them in her warm, throaty voice.

All of the squares in Savannah are surrounded by fine homes, but this house was one of the finest in the city. The Hamilton-Turner Mansion stirred Nancy's imagination in the strangest sort of way. Each day when she passed, she gazed at the house longingly. It was almost as if she had known the people who once lived there. When the realtor showed the house to her, she saw that its 10,000 square feet had been divided into eight apartment units with two bedrooms in each. When she bought it in March of 1991, she wished she could restore it all at once, but with the size of the house she realized she would have to do so a little at a time. Nancy Hillis shares the story of her experiences.

"First I began to work on the downstairs apartments as each lease was up. I lived in the house and made friends with one of the tenants, a young lady who ran her court-reporting business out of her apartment upstairs.

"Kelly was a nice girl and someone to talk to. One winter evening about dusk, just after I began restoring the second floor on the north side of the house, I thought I heard the sound of children's voices. They seemed to come from the third floor above me. Suddenly they stopped and it occurred to me that perhaps they had drifted up from out on the street. I must have only imagined it as coming from upstairs. It was about a month before I heard something again. That afternoon I was certain I heard children's giggles coming from above my head. I wondered how Kelly could work when her clients brought their children along with them, but that was her business.

"When someone else vacated, I moved to the other side of the house for a while and began to supervise plastering and repairs there. I pretty much wrote off my observations about Kelly's apartment as none of my business.

"Meanwhile I was growing more interested in the history of the house and the family who had lived there, searching the microfilm files of early newspapers for stories about the Hamiltons. The house was built about

1873 by a very prominent Savannah citizen named William Pugh Hamilton who had started out with a jewelry business and became head of the electric company and president of a large bank. He was highly respected—really one of the most prominent men in the city. The Hamiltons' six children occupied the top floor, with their nanny, and he had made the whole area suitable for the children putting a pool table up there for their amusement.

"It is my impression that after his first wife died, Hamilton married Sarah, the widow of his brother, who had been killed in the Civil War," continued Nancy Hillis.

"It was several weeks before I went back to the north side of the house to continue work restoring it. The first evening I clearly heard the sound of a ball rolling above me and, recalling my tenant's blonde cocker spaniel named Kramer, I dismissed it as the dog playing. A few days later I was certain that the sounds above me were not only of balls striking each other but of children giggling. I had seen Kelly, who lived upstairs, leave the house earlier, and when I heard the front door opening, I called, 'Kelly, is that you?'

"'Yes,' she said. 'I've just been out to get groceries.' She put the bags down at the foot of the stairs and looked at me inquiringly.

"'Kelly, I was sure you were upstairs from all the noise, and that one of your clients had brought their children with them. Do you ever hear any really odd sounds up there?'

"'You mean do I hear giggling and pool balls breaking?'

"'That's exactly what I mean.'

"'Oh, yes. Often.'

"'And you're not afraid?'

"'No. It has always seemed a cheerful sound.'

"I stared at her in surprise, but her attitude was at least reassuring. Continuing my research at the library, I discovered an interesting story in the *Savannah Morning News*. The headlines read, 'Mr. Hamilton's Children Were a Bit Rambunctious Last Night.' The story went on to relate that in the middle of the Hamiltons' party the kids got bored and hurled pool balls downstairs, hitting two of the guests. One guest was taken to the hospital, where he received head stitches.

"Upstairs where the children used to stay, I looked around me. 'I know you're here,' I said, thinking, I might as well confront whatever it was.

"'And I hope you don't mind my being here.'

"From then on the childish voices were much less muffled, and I could hear them calling out, 'Momma! Poppa!'

"Late one afternoon, a friend had been working with me here at the house in the gift shop we once had downstairs. The light outside was just beginning to fade when she ran up from the shop very frightened.

"'Nancy! Nancy!' she cried out, 'I simply can't work in this house anymore.' And as she hurried down the front steps to her car, she called back, 'An orange pool ball just came from upstairs and rolled down the steps to the shop. I'm not going back down there to work!'"

Nancy Hillis threw up her hands in a gesture of amazement. "It seems impossible for such a thing to happen. That ball would have to roll through a twenty-foot hallway, take a right turn, go down eighteen steps to the third floor, then travel down another twenty-foot hall, turn right again at the landing, and continue bumping down eighteen more steps. She told me that she could hear that pool ball rolling down the hall as it approached her, every moment coming closer and closer.

"'I clearly heard it strike first one step and then another,' she said, when she came back to get her paycheck. 'Then the sound grew louder and more distinct until that orange pool ball was rolling straight toward me. It stopped only inches from my feet.'"

Do the rambunctious spirits of the Hamilton children still troop back from another world? The Hamilton-Turner Mansion on Lafayette Square is now a luxury bed and breakfast, each room with its own distinct character and charm. But don't be surprised if you are an overnight guest there sometime and hear unusual sounds. Some say they have heard childish voices saying, "Papa, Papa!" Others are sure they've heard the sharp crack of a pool ball and then its thump, thump, thump down one riser after another of the stairs until it drops upon the floor of the front hall. It might even roll gently through the hall until it reaches your feet. After all, it has happened.

How ironic that this prominent Savannah gentleman, president of an electric company and a bank, may be remembered even more because of the specter of a lonely, resentful son hurling pool balls at his father's guests.

* * * * * *

The Hamilton-Turner Inn, at 330 Abercorn Street, is now a Victorian bed and breakfast, owned by Charlie and Sue Strickland. For information, phone 912-233-1833.

SECRET OF FOLEY HOUSE
Foley House Inn, Savannah, Georgia

. . . .

What better destination for a wedding trip than this house with a lingering touch of the macabre from the past? The Foley House is said to be one of the most romantic inns in the country, and guests soon find themselves caught up in its delightful ambience. They are surrounded by gleaming Federal period furniture, richly colored burgundy walls, magnificent crystal chandeliers, soft music, and the warm glow of the firelight.

While the guests sip wine and enjoy tiny hot crabmeat hors d'oeuvres and other delicacies, host Philip Jenkins pauses at each table to greet his guests. Then he settles himself at the baby grand piano and begins to weave a mood of enchantment. His fingers glide without pausing from "When You Wish upon a Star" into one romantic melody after another. The setting is characteristic of the elegance of Savannah and successfully transports visitors from the harried worlds of Atlanta, New York, or Detroit to the graceful tempo of a century ago. Time means little here.

It is a balmy February evening, and some guests have taken their wine outdoors and are sitting in the small private courtyards behind the house. I wonder why a woman standing in the hall at the foot of the stairs is shivering slightly. She seems to feel something more than the ordinary chill of evening in the air as she draws a light jacket about her shoulders. Then she looks around her to see where the cold air is coming from. The place where the stairs are now was once a common wall, and I too had felt a gust of chill air along there but a few minutes later found it no longer noticeable.

It was 1896 when Honora Foley began the building of this house as a

If the walls of the Foley House could talk, they might tell us a secret.

way to lift her from her deep gloom over the death of her husband. The life of a widow can be very lonely, so she decided to keep "paying guests." Of course, a single woman cannot be too careful, and she did her best to screen the men. A gentleman friend of hers often warned her, saying, "Honora, if you rent to the wrong sort of fellow, you could have trouble with his behavior or with getting him out of here."

But Honora was vary careful, and for several years all went well. Then a most attractive man arrived; she knew little about him other than what he told her. He pleaded with her to rent him a room, just for a month or two, while he did business in Savannah, and she gave in. He would never say exactly what his business was, which disturbed her. Soon she began to notice that he was becoming more and more familiar, and one night she awoke to see him bending over her bed, his face not far from her own. Panic-stricken, she seized the brass candlestick beside her bed and dealt him a blow to the temple.

He did not stir, and she had no doubt that he was dead. Mrs. Foley stepped back with a little moan of distress. As we can imagine, it is not easy for a well-bred lady to get rid of a dead body in the house. Her first thought was to bury him in the garden. Isn't that what people always did in books? But what would her neighbors think of her sudden interest in gardening? And had the books ever given the proper depth to dig?

Abandoning that idea, she dressed hurriedly and went out to awaken a gentleman friend who lived close by. It was not yet daylight. He had befriended her ever since she had moved in, even rooming in her house briefly while hurricane damage to his own was being repaired. He had never said so, but a friend of hers who had met him while he stayed in the house had said it was obvious that he was quite smitten with her. Had he declared his intentions, it would have been awkward, for how could a *lady* like herself marry a man who was only a bricklayer, even if he was well off. But she was right about trusting him now, for even in this dreadful predicament he did not hesitate to help her with her problem. No investigation is on record, and the secret of how a body had been quietly disposed of was not revealed during Mrs. Foley's lifetime.

A half-century or more passed. When the house did divulge its secret, it was not through the new owner's discovering a secret tunnel or stumbling upon a yellowed diary from the past that contained the story. It was after the small 1850 townhouse next door was purchased so that it might be combined with the adjacent Foley House to provide a more spacious bed and breakfast that a portion of the brick common wall between the small house and the Foley House was removed to provide space for a stairway and an entrance into the smaller building. As the brick common wall between the two houses was cut through, a grim discovery was made.

The remodeler discovered a hollow space in the wall of the Foley House, and within it was the skeleton of a man. At the time he was entombed in the wall, his age was estimated at about fifty years. Since we are unable to communicate with either Mrs. Foley or her friend the bricklayer (if, in truth, it was he who opened and then bricked over the common wall), we shall never be certain of the reason for this grisly interment. However, most of us will agree there is nothing like a shared secret to cement intimacy!

And as to the chill in the hall near the stairs? It is not unusual for people to experience it even today.

. . . . . .

The Foley House Inn, at 14 Hull Street in the heart of Savannah, has been called one of the most romantic bed and breakfast houses in the country. For information, phone 912-232-6622

River's End Restaurant and Lounge, Thunderbolt, Georgia

• •

He had always wanted his own business, and now Michael Strickland had it. It was a restaurant with a romantic setting under the moonlit harbor sky unmatched anywhere in Savannah. Diners at River's End enjoy watching the lights on passing luxury craft glide gently past on the Intracoastal Waterway. The restaurant is tucked away in the quaint fishing village of Thunderbolt, but there is a "presence" here that the new owner hadn't counted on.

More than 250 years ago Thunderbolt was an abandoned Indian settlement, but miles across the ocean a different future was being shaped. An English earl was signing papers to grant American colonist families five hundred acres each to settle in Georgia and pursue the making of silk. In 1734 there were six hundred people in the entire colony when ten families arrived from England and settled at Thunderbolt. Now it is a community of about fifteen hundred residents, seven miles from downtown Savannah.

"Our people live in a different world at a slower pace, and they have successfully resisted being annexed by the city," says Michael. "I like it here because everyone knows each other and there is a strong sense of community.

"People ask me how the name of this town came to be. According to the Indian legend, the settlement was named after a bolt of lightning was seen to strike the ground during a terrible storm. The following morning everyone gathered in amazement to gaze at a spring bubbling up from where the

lightning struck. The water has flowed from it for years, and the well at the site of that spring is still used.

"Of course this area belonged to the Indians, and I've always heard that in places built on top of a burying ground the spirits of the Indians were still about. When anything happens here, it is natural to wonder if they sometimes return. One of the first nights I was open, I was here with the cashier closing up. Suddenly we both heard the door to the kitchen open and close. We were alone in the building. The rest of the staff had all left, and the entrances had been locked behind them. We were both very concerned about the sound of the door opening, so I called the police, and they came out and checked thoroughly. They found the doors still locked from the inside and no one there.

"For a while all was peaceful, until one morning I came in early and found dishes scattered all over the floor. The odd thing is that nothing was broken. When our staff arrived, they were as shocked as I had been.

"But to return to our strange events, we began to find another phenomenon. Tables that we had set up with place settings and glasses perfectly arranged were completely disarranged. They were 'all messed up' and could be a source of embarrassment if a waitperson conducted a party to a table looking as if it had been set by a mischievous toddler. This became a real headache.

"Finally one of the waiters made a suggestion, and we decided to try it. 'Before we leave tonight, let's set up a table just for "him,"' the waiter suggested. 'Let whoever it is know we are friendly.' We placed a very nice meal on the table for our 'spirit,' with glasses and silverware meticulously arranged in their proper places. The next morning every bit of the food had disappeared. This act of cordiality seemed to have its effect, for the mischievous activities of the ghost have been seen only rarely since. Occasionally we do have the burglar alarm system go off inexplicably, and when we check, nothing is found that could have triggered it."

Another minor incident Michael relates is when he or another member of the staff feels someone breathing on the back of his neck. "But no event ever occurs of a hostile nature," says Michael. The ghost undoubtedly enjoys observing the preparation of food at the River's End and watching egrets, porpoises, otters, and other wildlife on the Intracoastal Waterway. The wildlife is undoubtedly an important part of this ghost's Indian heritage.

This restaurant and lounge is named River's End because River Drive, which turns off Victory Drive, comes to an end right in front of it. In the forty years since the restaurant has been open, it has received countless awards and been featured in many magazines. It serves dinner only (phone, 912-354-2973).

THE HAUNTED MARSHALL HOUSE
Savannah, Georgia

. . . .

When Sue and Richard Martin arrived, they planned to stay in one of Savannah's many attractive bed and breakfasts—but they had not anticipated the annual St. Patrick's Day celebration. Every place they called was full. Tired, they at last drove down East Broughton Street past the imposing Marshall House hotel and decided to stop. Surprised by a courteous greeting from the doorman, a custom out of the past, they waited hopefully at the desk in the lobby.

"We have only one room left, sir, said the desk clerk, and it is in the adjoining building. We call it the Florida Quarter. Would that be satisfactory?"

"Yes," said Richard with a sigh of relief. He had begun to wonder whether they would find accommodations anywhere in the city.

"Would you care to see the room first?" asked the clerk.

"Oh I'm sure it will be fine," said Sue, eager to change into blue jeans and comfortable shoes.

"We're from near Gettysburg, Pennsylvania. Does the Marshall House have any Civil War history connected with it?" asked Richard.

"Oh, yes." said the young woman. "This building was occupied by Union troops under General William Sherman, and it was also a Union hospital until the end of the war. I wouldn't be surprised if you met the ghost of General Sherman in one of these halls," she said.

"I think that is highly unlikely," Richard replied with a wry smile. He was a doctor and not at all a superstitious man. His wife, Sue, owned an antique shop. They were in their early fifties and their children grown.

"I wonder where those fellows did their surgery," asked Richard.

"We can ask tomorrow and see if anyone knows," said Sue. "I can't imagine them having operating tables with wheels or gurneys to take patients to different parts of the building. Perhaps a room on each floor? But primitive—not the kind of operating room equipment we visualize today."

"The Confederacy seldom had anesthetics and sometimes even the Union was short of them," said Dr. Martin with a grimace. The thought of men enduring such suffering and dying with no modern instruments or anesthetics bothered him.

The Martins were soon settled in the Florida Quarter. They were changing to walk along the riverfront when Richard Martin suddenly stopped to listen.

"Do you hear the sound of a typewriter coming from the room next to us?" he asked.

"No, and it is very unlikely," she said.

"Why not?"

"Because everyone uses computers now, and they are much quieter."

"Someone could use a typewriter if he wanted to, couldn't he?"

"Of course, but it wouldn't make much sense. Let's walk down instead of taking the elevator."

Seeing the ladies' room when they got downstairs, Sue said, "I'll just run in a minute." When she entered, she found all the stalls closed. She waited and then finally knocked on the door of one of them. No one answered. To her surprise not one of them was occupied. They were enclosed from floor to ceiling and locked from the inside! She wondered how the occupants had managed to get out.

They stopped at the desk to report it and received an embarrassed look from the desk clerk who had rented them the room. "I'm so sorry. This will be taken care of immediately. Let me know if it occurs again."

"What does she mean, if it occurs again?" said Sue. "Is this a frequent event?" They stared at each other in bewilderment. The doorman graciously opened the door.

While they wandered along the waterfront enjoying the mild weather, they window-shopped and munched pralines; they purchased a model

ship, and Sue selected a book of ghost stories. Despite the St. Patrick's Day celebrants, they were finally able to get a table at Huey's restaurant. When they finished with dinner, they headed up the stone steps of the bluff to their car.

Back at the Marshall House, Sue dozed off almost immediately and Richard turned off the bedside lamp; but for him sleep did not come. He decided to go out to the car and bring in a book of his own to read. Returning, he walked along the halls of the hotel for a few minutes studying the historic pictures decorating the walls until he realized that he was not certain where he was. And it was almost midnight.

He had just decided that he was in the old part of the building when he heard the soft sound of footsteps descending the stairs.

Thinking he would wait until whoever it was had passed before he mounted the steps to his own floor, he stood beside the corridor wall about ten feet from the stairwell. A man approached from the floor above, his arms stretched behind him carrying the head of a stretcher, while another man brought up the rear. They seemed to be carrying a body on the stretcher, and Dr. Martin decided that the two men must be hospital attendants.

It was strange, for although he saw them, he could not make out their faces clearly. Perhaps because he was unable to take his eyes off the stretcher with the long form covered by a white sheet. By the length of the body from head to foot, he judged it to be a man of more than average height. In fact it was someone about his own height and build.

He heard the low voices of the men.

"Guess we won't be bothered by the complaining of Wright any longer," said one of the men to the other, in a strangely muffled, faraway voice, as he nodded at the form under the sheet.

"Yes. It's down to the basement with him," answered the other as they rounded the end of the rail and started down the next flight with their burden.

"This basement gives me the creeps," said the man nearest Martin.

"You mean the bones? They take 'em out pretty often."

"Not often enough for me," muttered the other, and then they disappeared into the thick darkness of the stairwell. All sounds ceased, and Martin was surprised at how rapidly his heart was beating. Soon he heard the footsteps coming back up, and he froze. The two men he had just seen descending had returned. The empty stretcher was under one attendant's arm. The other joined him, and then to Richard's horror they extended the stretcher toward him, gesturing for him to get on! Despite himself, he felt some strange force drawing him toward the macabre scene.

"No. No!" he gasped only to see them vanish!

Shaken, Richard Martin hurried back to his room. He slept poorly. The next morning at breakfast he asked one of the wait staff, "Is there anything interesting down in the hotel basement?"

The server looked at him strangely as if considering how to respond. "Nothing I know of, sir. Of course that is where bits of human bone were found while we were remodeling here, but they are all gone now."

"A man or a woman?" asked Richard.

"I think they determined it was a rather tall man, sir," said the waitperson, his eyes averted. Richard was convinced the man had seen something.

"Are bones the normal thing to discover in Savannah basements?" he asked.

"Oh, no sir!" came the response. "But this hotel and many of the houses here in the city were hospitals for soldiers during the Union occupation." He coughed. "Unfortunately not all the patients recovered."

"Is this really breakfast table talk?" asked Mrs. Martin.

"I'm sorry, dear. We'll change the subject," said her husband.

"Do you know anything about any ghosts here in the hotel?" he suddenly blurted out to the waiter, surprising himself.

"I wouldn't be able to tell you about that, sir, for I'm not here at night, but some would have you believe that there are ghosts around every corner—going up and down the stairs, clicking away on the keys of an old typewriter behind the door of a room in the annex. In fact, the room from which the typing is reportedly heard belonged to Joel Chandler Harris, author of the Uncle Remus stories. Now that's an interesting bit of history for you." Mrs. Martin, who had turned pale, rose quickly and left the table.

"Sorry, sir. I hope I haven't upset your wife."

"I don't think so," replied Dr. Martin. But he resolved to check on Sue.

"Mr. Harris lived in the annex," the server continued, "and he wrote many of his stories here. In fact he met and married a Savannah girl. There were parties for the young lady and her friends at the hotel, and some say that is why the doors in the ladies' restroom keep locking."

Dr. Martin excused himself; when he reached their room, his wife was packing. It was with difficulty that he cajoled her into staying in the beautifully restored old hotel, at least for the St. Patrick's Day Celebration. He finally persuaded her, saying, "My dear, think what you will have to tell your friends when we do return to Gettysburg."

He already knew that he wanted to stay another night. He thought of stationing himself in the basement near midnight and waiting for the two stretcher-bearers to come down the stairs. And then he realized that he was taking this entirely too far. It was one thing to think he had seen something supernatural—it was another to get squarely in the middle of it and perhaps wind up on that stretcher himself! He should not permit superstition to take charge of his life. He would forget what he had seen—or not seen—

and he and Sue would have the most enjoyable St. Patrick's Day of their lives. But what about that night—after his wife was asleep—what harm would it do to go back and wait for the stretcher-bearers?

. . . . . .

The Marshall House, at 123 East Broughton Street, is an impressive hotel, with the luxury of the present and the amenities of the past. For information, phone 912-644-789.

MYSTERY AT THE MOON RIVER
Moon River Restaurant and Brewery, Savannah, Georgia

· ·

hy do so many places in Savannah have a reputation for being haunted? There are a dozen possible answers. Important historical events have happened here. Pierre and Jean Lafitte, Edward Teach, Calico Jack Rackham, Captain Charles Vane, and other pirates, from all over the world once walked the streets of this city. A group of hot-blooded revolutionaries organized here, calling themselves the Liberty Boys, and immediately found themselves in conflict with their angry fathers who had been born in England and were loyal to the king. Stories of suffering and personal tragedy are everywhere. Famous figures in history visited this city—men like Winfield Scott, the Marquis de Lafayette, and John James Audubon. Perhaps these are some of the reasons Savannah is said to have so many ghosts. This story is about a couple who would soon find out.

Glenn and Iris Cranston left Atlanta about midmorning and arrived in Savannah late one afternoon. This was their honeymoon destination, and they were going to try to experience all of the city's cultural and culinary delights at once!

First they headed for the riverfront, and then, since they had not been able to decide on a restaurant for dinner, they climbed the steps back up to Factors Walk. Crossing the street, they began to stroll along West Bay Street, and Glenn began to sing softly.

"What is that song?" said Iris. "It sounds so familiar."

"It should be. It's 'Moon River.'" In fact the city renamed a stretch of river between Pigeon Island and Burnside Island "Moon River" in Johnny Mercer's honor. Seems Mercer, who was a native of Savannah and had a house on Monterey Square, could see the path of moonlight on that river from his house and he loved it. Part of the song goes "Moon River, wider than a mile. I'm crossin' you in style some day."

"I like it, but why did you happen to sing it now?"

"The sign back there—didn't you see it?"

"The restaurant—of course! It said, Moon River Brewing Company. Let's walk back there and look at the menu, Glenn," Iris suggested. And that was the way they happened to choose the restaurant. The manager was glad to show them the beautiful features of this early building, and he gave them a tour of the second floor. It was designed by William Jay, whose architecture is characterized by classical references and a bold geometry. Jay used curved surfaces for walls, doors, and sometimes even for the entire front of a building. Glenn and Iris Cranston were fascinated.

Returning to the dining room, while they waited for their food, Iris decided to go to the ladies' room and reached for her rucksack.

"Oh my. How careless of me. I think I must have left my bag somewhere during our tour of the upstairs. I will be back in a few minutes, Glenn."

She had no sooner left than the manager paused at the Cranston table and spoke to Glenn. "Did I tell you folks about the ghost while we were on our little tour? Most people who visit the Moon River for a meal probably never know this place has a reputation for being haunted," said he. "Much of the activity takes place up on the second floor where we were a few minutes ago."

"What sort of activity?" asked Glenn.

"Well, according to what the staff reports, it's the sound of footsteps, voices—something being dragged across the floor."

"Hmm . . . and who do people think that it is?"

"I don't really know. Some say the ghost of the pirate, Jean Lafitte. Others tell the story of a Civil War bummer who forcibly entered this place and was killed here."

There is much more to the Moon River restaurant than meets the eye. Some say it's the spirit of a Civil War soldier!

"A bummer?"

"Yes. That was the term for a deserter from either army—they were renegades and plunderers." As the manager said this, Iris returned to the table.

"Well, that's a grisly notion, and I'm not sure I believe in ghosts. When has the apparition been seen recently?" But the manager was already excusing himself and was on his way to another table as Iris sat down. She put her hand on Glenn's arm.

"Perhaps I can answer your question," she said. "The last time it happened was just a few minutes ago."

Glenn looked shocked. "What do you know about it?" he asked and saw for the first time that her hands were trembling.

"My bag was on the floor where I had left it. I picked it up and started back, and I had almost reached the hall when I saw the tall figure of a man blocking the doorway. He stood facing me, arms folded, seemingly with no intention of moving. Then he stepped forward, reaching out for me. I was really scared, Glenn. I couldn't get by on either side. Whether I escaped by going past him or through him I will probably never know."

"Incredible!" said Glenn. "Darling, are you sure you are all right now?" She nodded.

"People say they've seen the apparition of a man standing with his arms folded. You saw him too?"

"I certainly did," said Iris.

"They were renovating here a few years ago and found bones at the bottom of a well in the basement," said Glenn. "The bones were judged to be from the Civil War era. Of course the well was not in use and was cemented over. I'm sorry about your experience. You look pale, dear. Let's forget about ghosts. After all, they can't really harm anyone. Did you like that song I was singing?"

"Sing it again." Glenn obliged.

"Now, what are the rest of the words to that song?" Iris asked when they were back out on West Bay Street.

"Do you want me to sing it now?"

"Why not? It is romantic."

"And just the right song for us," said Glenn, putting his arm around her waist and beginning to sing very softly as they walked along.

· · · · · ·

The Moon River Brewing Company is a casual, pleasant restaurant and brewery, with some fine architectural details—as well as a ghost! It is located at 21 West Bay Street. For reservations or information, call 912-447-0943.

. . . .

F
ew people, outside of Georgia, have ever heard of the Altamaha, a dark, mysterious river that winds past the town of
Darien through a maze of marshes, concealed creeks, and shadowy cypress swamps in the southern part of the state. Somewhere in its depths is said to lurk a mysterious creature similar
to the Loch Ness Monster. Nor is this the only such report on the American coast, or other coasts.

One of the most famous accounts was that of the appearance of the
Gloucester, Massachusetts, sea serpent. It was seen for a full two weeks by
hundreds off Cape Ann in August of 1817. Observers described it as being
dark brown and fifty to one hundred feet long, with the head of a rattle-
snake and a body as "thick as half a barrel." Like a snake, it had no limbs. Its
head rose out of the water, and it was estimated to move at about thirty
miles an hour.

And then there was that most fearsome of all reported sea monsters, the
Kraken, the name Swedes gave to giant squids, which have been said to attack and even overturn ships at sea. Some of these creatures weighed nearly
a ton. The most recent sighting came in 1875, when a giant squid was seen
locked in mortal combat with a sperm whale off the coast of Zanzibar. In
the 1980s and 1990s several sea serpents have been reported—the Champ at
Lake Champlain, New York; Ogopogo at Okanagan Lake in British Columbia; and now the Altamaha sea serpent in the Altamaha River near
Darien, Georgia. All three share startling resemblances.

In periodic, breathtaking encounters, the Altamaha serpent has been reported by fishermen from Darien as far south as the waters near St. Augus-

tine and Jacksonville, Florida. Of course we all start out as skeptics, but since species deemed extinct for millennia are discovered each year, why not sea serpents?

Cathleen Williamson of the *Darien News* writes of a crab fisherman, Ralph DeWitt, who was on his daily rounds checking his traps in the sound just before heading into the Carneghan River. Steering into the river's mouth, DeWitt glanced to his left at the entrance and saw what he thought was a dock piling. On second thought, he decided, it might be trash draped around a buoy.

"I thought I would just run over in the boat and take a look at it," said he. "To my surprise, I discovered it was alive!" Approaching the object, he was about forty feet away when it suddenly dipped down into the water. Its body, a foot or more in diameter, arched up and with swift undulating loops propelled itself through the water toward the channel.

"Did I really see that?" DeWitt asked himself in astonishment as he headed out into the river to check his traps. He looked back several times to see if the serpentine creature would surface again and was about to write it off as an illusion when he turned and saw the eel-shaped head break the water once more and come up dripping. Cautiously he motored toward it, staying on the far side of the river, then edged around behind it.

About two boat lengths away now, he watched the large head dip into the water, its sleek brown snakelike body rolling up above the surface. Then abruptly it plunged down, submerging itself in the depths of the river.

"I've seen sturgeon, porpoise, manatee, but never a creature like this before," said the veteran crabber. DeWitt is one of many fishermen who are out scanning the water daily, more at home on it than on land. Sightings have come from many witnesses. Mariners, scientists, lawmen, and even casual passersby on Highway 17 and Interstate 95 near Brunswick, unaware of the previously reported appearances, have stopped to report seeing this creature.

Early explorers heard stories about the Ogopogo and the Altamaha from the Indians more than two centuries ago. Those were the days when canoe trips across lakes and on rivers were the common modes of transportation for everyone.

Darien News writer Cathleen Williamson repeats another sighting story told to her by Harvey Blackman, a veteran fisherman from Brunswick. He was standing on a floating dock when "it was rocked by a great wave and a monstrous creature fifteen to twenty feet long, its girth the size of a man's body, came up near the dock. The color was a slick grayish brown and when it raised out of the water, its head was the shape of a snake's."

And then there is Barry Prescott. As he tells what he saw, his blue eyes are serious and convincing. This tall, well-built six-footer with gray hair has lived in the Darien area for many years, and much of his life has revolved around the sea. During his boyhood Barry's summers were spent with his grandmother on the west coast of England adjoining Cornwall. We went up to Scotland to Loch Ness every year, he says, "and I loved the mystery of it all, but we never saw anything." An Englishman turned Georgian, he gazes out over the water from the bridge on I-95 near Brunswick, and this is what he recalls.

"When I came to Georgia, I lived near the water and spent eight or nine hours a day on it for seven years. I made a living fishing for catfish and blue crab. Often I was the only person on the water for miles around. You notice anything unusual when you're out there alone for hours at a time.

"I have had two sightings of this creature. The first was in 1980, and that day I was driving along on I-95 and noticed a major disturbance in the water. I reversed to see what was happening, stopped, and got out of the car. This river was one I had fished many times, and I remembered that over on the left-hand side there was a large, soft mudbank beneath the water.

"My guess was that whatever was causing the water to churn so violently in that area was something that was having difficulty getting off of the mudbank. Then I saw a brownish shape break the water. Its skin was coarse and as mottled as an elephant's. I watched for twelve or fifteen minutes while the creature was propelling itself ahead with a kind of desperate undulating movement. As it did so, tons of mud were spurting up, splashing the surface of its reptilian body.

"The disturbance was about fifteen feet wide and thirty or forty feet long. It was on both sides of the body, and the movement was so furious it appeared that the creature was in a state of panic. I could see the ridge of its long backbone, for about half the body was above water. It appeared to be stranded and was thrashing forward and slightly sideways. The deep channel was about twenty feet away, and it finally reached this and disappeared. I never thought to be afraid, for it all took place so quickly and had nothing to do with me."

Barry Prescott's nextdoor neighbor stood watching with him just as astonished as Prescott. "It doesn't fit the description of anything I've ever seen," he said.

Prescott's second sighting did not occur until about a dozen years later. "It was in August of 1992 when I was out in my boat. Suddenly there the creature was, its appearance just as I remembered—the large snakelike head, the long neck, and the humps with the water in between. The sun was low on the horizon when I saw that strange, prehistoric silhouette, with its great loops and the head held high. It was perhaps a hundred yards away and about thirty or forty feet long. That startling glimpse lasted only a few seconds before the creature surged forward and submerged.

"I'm sure there are many people who have seen the Altamaha sea serpent. They just don't want to admit it. There are times when something is so bizarre that we are tempted to convince ourselves we never really saw it. As we talked, Prescott leaned on the bridge rail, scratched his chin reflectively, and stared down at the dark, swift-flowing waters of the Altamaha.

"In the meantime, it is a mystery," he continued. "It has probably been out there for millions of years, perhaps much longer than we humans have. I just hope to see it again someday."

THE LIGHT IN THE CEMETERY
Christ Church, St. Simons Island, Georgia

. . . .

She loved the sound of the sea, the wind through the live oaks, the songs the blacks sang as they picked the sea island cotton, and she loved her husband. Now, for the first time in her life, she was desperately afraid. She had never felt this ill before. Was she going to die? Why was her room so dark?

"Go check the supply of beeswax candles, Wanda," she said to her maid. "If we are running low, you must go to the storeroom and bring more. I must not run out when night comes."

When she heard the sound of a carriage and men's voices outdoors, she knew the doctor had arrived from Brunswick. Her husband had gone out to greet him. Now they were entering the downstairs hall and coming up the stairs. Her room was growing darker. Why didn't someone hurry and light more candles so that it would not be so gloomy? Did they think that because she was sick she wanted to shut out the sun? She dreaded dusk, for after that came night.

The servant girl was back. "Open the shutters wider, Wanda. Open them, I say!"

"But m'am, dusk is coming down."

"Not in this room. I won't let it! Go and get another lamp." A moment after the girl had left to do the bidding of her mistress, there was a knock at the bedroom door.

"May I come in, Mrs. Lanier?"

"Certainly." The doctor was accompanied by her husband.

New in the Brunswick area, the doctor was a man in his early thirties, and he seemed awed by the great house and its beauty. Rachel Lanier, looking very small and very feverish, lay in the middle of an enormous four-poster bed with a ruffled canopy. As soon as he saw her, the doctor realized there was little he could do. It was yellow fever. She might linger on another day or go that very night. How lovely she was, with her blonde hair, silky brows, and fair skin. He silently cursed his inability to save her.

When the two men left the room, he inquired, "Mr. Lanier, I must ask whether the rector has been here to call." Lanier shook his head, and the doctor stroked his beard thoughtfully.

"Then you may wish to summon him."

James Lanier gazed at the doctor disbelievingly, then assented. He sent a young servant boy to the vicarage, returned to his wife's room, and sat down beside the bed as yet another lamp was brought in.

"What did he say, James?"

"That he thought you would be better soon, Rachel."

"No he didn't! I want to know the truth, James. Tell me what he really said."

"He said . . . he said," her husband's voice broke, and he turned his face away from his wife, for his eyes were filled with tears.

"He said I'm going to die! That's what he said, didn't he? Oh, I'm so afraid!" She began sobbing, and, heedless of contagion, her husband rushed to her and held her in his arms. But her outburst had exhausted her, and soon she fell asleep.

The rector arrived that evening. George Tindall was thin, with gray hair, and his congregation found him dignified but kindly. He was a man who tried his best to do his duty. When Mrs. Lanier awoke and saw Father Tindall standing beside her bed, her hand went involuntarily to her throat and she gave a small startled cry. He started to take her hand in his own in an effort to comfort her, but she shrank back.

"My dear," he was able to say, "I am sure you have nothing to worry about."

"Nothing to worry about, sir? I am going to die!"

"I hope that will not happen, but if it should, you will find that everlasting joy and peace await you."

Somewhere in the cemetery behind this lovely old church is a grave where the light of a candle never goes out.

"Joy? My joy is here. I shall find nothing but the darkness of the grave!"

"I am distressed to hear you say that."

"And will I then get to heaven?"

Father Tindall was taken off guard by this direct approach. "My dear, if you have sincerely confessed your sins and asked Christ to forgive you, he will welcome you with the greatest love that you can possibly imagine. And you will live in his presence forever."

"Christ? Why would I want to live with him, Father? I don't even know him! All I know is that I am going down into terrible darkness alone!" The rector had no time to respond, for she seemed to recollect something and, turning away, spoke to her husband.

"Oh James, I shall never get to wear all my new dresses made for the Christmas parties in Savannah!" And with that Rachel began to weep inconsolably.

Suddenly her eyes grew wide and frightened, and she reached for her husband's hand. "James, promise me that you will not let me lie out in that cemetery in the dark," she pleaded. "I promise," he said, and her eyes closed as she drifted off to sleep. An hour later Rachel was gone.

Each evening thereafter, at dusk, her widowed husband, true to his word, set out in his carriage to go to her grave in St. Simons Christ Church cemetery. He would first kneel beside the grave and pray for Rachel, for he believed that the prayers of the living would continue to help the dead. Then he would bring a candle from his breast pocket and light it in front of the young woman's headstone. And so this act of devotion was repeated for many years until Lanier himself became an invalid.

But they say that even after his death the candle flame has never gone out—that it still burns bright upon Rachel's grave at night. It flickers near the headstone but disappears before anyone quite succeeds in reaching it. No one at Christ Church will divulge the location of the grave.

. . . . . .

Christ Church is on the road to Fort Frederica. Built in 1820, this lovely historic church was the site of several services conducted by John and Charles Wesley. Daytime tours are available. For information, phone 912-638-8683.

BLOODTHIRSTY ABRAHAM
St. Simons Island, Georgia

· ·

When Jane Moers Farmer moved to St. Simons in 1983, she looked forward to enjoying its mild climate, palms, and tropical flowers. Moss-draped trees enhance the setting of the homes and throw a perpetual cloak of eerie twilight around the old gravestones in Christ Church cemetery.

"Of the large settled Georgia islands, we had always heard St. Simons was one of the loveliest and most mysterious," says Mrs. Farmer. "We found it lovely but, of course, I was prepared to take superstitions lightly."

A no-nonsense New Englander who is a direct descendant of John Alden, Jane Farmer is also a scholar. She set out to research St. Simons's history and learned that the island has seen Spanish galleons and colonial explorers, pirate ships and plunderers, Puritans and Scottish Highlanders, planters and English gunboats, along with slave ships smuggling in their precious black cargo.

A respected St. Simons historian and speaker, Jane Moers Farmer not only knows the island's past but has had some amazing experiences of her own.

"The first time anything that I really couldn't explain happened was as I was leaving a meeting at the St. Simons Elementary School," says Farmer. "It was about nine-thirty at night that I backed out of the school driveway and suddenly braked when my taillights illuminated three men walking in the road. They were dressed in dark robes and wearing broad-brimmed hats. From the early sketches I had seen, they looked exactly like Franciscan priests. I drove very slowly and in my side-view mirror I could still see them back there, robes flapping in the wind, as they walked along the road in the moonlight.

"Of course, I knew that during the time the Spanish occupied this island there had been a Franciscan monastery here, and priests were a common sight in the late 1600s. This trio was heading purposefully in the direction of the sea. Were they on their way to board, or perhaps to greet the dignitaries on, some Spanish galleon? In the brief moments that I watched this trio out of the past I felt a sense of indescribable awe. Although I attended other meetings at night at the school, I never glimpsed them on that road again.

"What else have I seen in the years I have lived here? I think the most impressive sight by far was the sailing vessel. I waked one misty, rainy morning just at daybreak and, rising, looked out the window. I couldn't believe my eyes, and I rubbed them with my fists. But there it was, *a sailing ship at anchor*. It was close to the bridge on upper Frederica Road near Epworth. When I reported it, I was amazed to learn that I was not the only one who had seen such a sight. Sailing vessels have been reported several times, and so sure are those who have seen them that they have made calls to both the St. Simons Police and the Fire Department."

Some have seen a single ship flying the skull and crossbones slipping in with the tide, a ship that is said to be the phantom ship of the bloodthirsty pirate Abraham Agramont. Many a time he raided the early missions along the Georgia and Florida coast, stealing chapel bells and crosses to melt down and recast for his artillery and ammunition. "Bloody Abraham," as they called him, and his crew plundered missions and murdered Indian converts in a string of coastal towns that the Spanish had settled.

Terrified by these attacks, the Spaniards gradually closed their missions in Georgia and moved southward, seeking protection from the better-garrisoned missions of Florida. Finding the Georgia towns undefended, Agramont and his men struck ever more boldly.

In the summer of 1682 he and five other pirate captains combined forces and raided the coast. Starting at St. Augustine, they sailed north, attacking Cumberland Island, where they stole four mission bells. Then they sailed on to Jekyll and St. Simons Islands, murdering and plundering as they went. Because of the pirates' own depraved characters and rebellious natures, they desecrated churches with filth and hacked off the hands, feet, and heads of sacred statues. It was four years before the pirates were defeated and no longer a threat to the islanders.

According to the story handed down from the mission towns, bloodthirsty Abraham Agramont and his crew were so wicked they can never rest—nor are they allowed to drop anchor or quench their thirst in any harbor. They are doomed to sail forever through the coastal creeks and inlets of St. Simons near the places they once plundered. And what of the sailing ship Mrs. Farmer saw at dawn on Upper Frederica Creek? Was it a fulfillment of the legend of Agramont? All we know is that vessels that prove to be "phantom ships" are still reported at St. Simons and and other of Georgia's Golden Isles.

"On a more romantic note, I am probably one of the few fortunate enough to have glimpsed 'Mary the Wanderer,'" says Jane Farmer. "She was the girl who died searching for her sweetheart who was lost in a storm. I am sure that I came upon her one windy, stormy night at the edge of the water, her lantern held high. The sight of the girl was accompanied by so sweet a fragrance in the air that I shall never forget it.

"I am not superstitious, but I have discovered St. Simons to be a place which not only has beauty, but mysteries to entice and intrigue for a lifetime."

. . . . . .

The scholarly Mrs. Farmer is the compiler of the history of Christ Episcopal Church, the oldest church on St. Simons Island, and is widely known for her island story presentations.

The Jekyll Island Club Hotel, Jekyll Island, Georgia

· ·

Two decades after the Civil War, an exclusive club was formed on one of Georgia's beautiful Golden Isles. It was called the Jekyll Island Club. The members were among the wealthiest and most powerful men in America, and all they sought was a place to enjoy the good life with their peers. Who would have thought that such a natural desire could lead to a haunting. A haunting that reportedly goes on to this day.

Young Richard Hayes had often heard of the Jekyll Island Club, the onetime playground of America's northern millionaires, and he had always longed to stay there. Now he was about to realize his dream. His wife, Amy, had suggested accompanying him, but this was a work trip needed to solve a business problem and he had told her, "We will go together some other time and enjoy it when I am not so busy."

As he drove through the entrance, he was impressed by his first view of the club. Its magnificent, rambling assemblage of turreted buildings and the magnolias, pines, and azaleas on the beautifully landscaped grounds that provided pleasant vistas were once seen by only a favored few. Some men would have sold their souls to be a member of this club, but membership here could not be bought. Each candidate had to have a sponsor, be judged worthy by other members' standards, and be elected by a board of directors who need cast only two negative ballots to reject a banker, corporate president, or distinguished government figure.

Richard Hayes, a descendant through certain vague connections of a famous early bridge builder and club member, Edmund Hayes, knew that for some years the club had been open to the general public, so he had called and made reservations. Now he waited with some discomfort before the desk clerk, noticing for the first time that his luggage looked a bit shabby. The clerk adjusted her glasses and seemed to stare down interminably at her list of rooms.

"Do you wish the annex? I could put you there," she said, looking up at him questioningly.

"That will be fine," he replied. Were the prices for the annex rooms more modest? he wondered. Had she been judging what to offer him by his appearance? Then he told himself that even if that were true, it was unimportant, for he was here to work and he could still enjoy the magnificent surroundings.

She gave him a pleasant smile. "How would you like Apartment Eight? That was once part of the suite belonging to Mr. Samuel Spencer. They bought their suites." She handed him a key.

"He was a railroad man, wasn't he?" asked Richard.

"Yes, and brilliant. He had a degree in civil engineering, and like a number of other Confederate veterans, after the war was over, he went into railroading. He became president of Southern Railway and was one of the few southerners ever invited to join the club. Members drew for their living quarters, and he was considered lucky to draw Apartment Eight, an especially bright and airy suite of rooms. Of course the apartments have all been divided, and Apartment Eight is only one large room now."

"That's very interesting. I shall tell my wife about staying in his room."

"I hope your stay there will be—uneventful."

"That is an unusual word to use. Is there any reason it shouldn't be?"

"Of course not. That's just a room in which people sometimes report strange things happening, that's all."

"What sort of things?"

"Oh, nothing serious. I shouldn't even have mentioned it."

"Are you implying a ghost?"

"Well, yes and no. Sometimes people find papers moved."

"How ridiculous. You may be sure I am the last person to believe in anything supernatural," Richard Hayes said with a brittle little laugh. "I must be able to test, weigh, and measure anything before I believe in it."

"I'm sure you're quite right," she agreed. "Are you an engineer too, sir, like Mr. Spencer was?"

"As a matter of fact I am not only an engineer but right now a very hungry one. Is there a good, moderately priced restaurant close by?" She gave him the names of several local places, whereupon, picking up his suitcase and briefcase, he headed for the annex and Apartment Eight. He found it to be a spacious room with two windows facing south and far more luxurious in its furnishings, carpeting, draperies and appointments than he had anticipated. But there was certainly nothing that suggested the supernatural about it.

Richard opened his briefcase and withdrew several manila folders bulging with papers and drawings. He planned to spend two, perhaps three days here at the club. In the quiet, undisturbed atmosphere he would work on several phases of a bold and innovative plan to present to his employer on his return. This room would serve as his temporary office, where no one had any call on his time and no one could glance even in passing at any of his papers. He placed his *Wall Street Journal* on a chair to read later and went out to a restaurant.

When he returned, he began working with his usual intense concentration, and before he knew it the alarm in his watch reminded him it was ten o'clock. It was his habit never to retire later than that hour, so that he might be fresh for work the next morning. His project was to have three phases, so he sorted the papers with great care labeling and arranging his preliminary drawings between the pages of text in the proper order. Then he divided it into three piles placing some china object from the room on the top of each. He was discouraged with the last drawing in pile two. As he studied it, somehow it did not link up smoothly with pile three and the final outcome of the process. Well, he would go over it again tomorrow.

He looked for his *Wall Street Journal* to read just before he went to sleep but was unable to lay hands upon it. Finally he discovered part of it on the floor between the wall and the bed. It was opened to the business news. Much to his bewilderment, the rest of the paper was in the wastebasket

Imagine a place like the prestigious Jekyll Island Club Hotel having a haunted room!

under a table. Beside one story, written in a bold hand, was the word "Shameful!" How very strange! Someone must have a master key to the rooms, he thought, and be determined to produce events that appeared supernatural. Ridiculous that people would go to such lengths, he said to himself irritatedly.

In the morning he put a "do not disturb" sign on his door and went down to the small deli on the porch for a light breakfast.

Entering his room, no more than forty-five minutes later, he was astonished to see several papers on the floor beside the table where he had placed his project piles. He glanced at them but found nothing missing, and, assuming the papers had been blown to the floor by air coming from an air-conditioning vent, he went back to work.

Returning from lunch, he discovered that the last drawing was missing from pile two. It was the one that he was dissatisfied with in the flow of his project. Well, it would turn up and he would work on it later, he decided.

The rest of the day and evening were devoted to rewriting and simplifying the explanation of his new idea. He realized only when the phone rang beside his bed about eleven-thirty that he had not called his wife as he had promised. Moreover it was his son's birthday and he had promised her to call him. "Tell him I will bring him something," he said and assured her he would call the child the next day.

The following morning, when he returned from breakfast, his room was in a shocking state. Papers were strewn on the bureau, the chairs, even among his rumpled bedclothes. He was consumed with fury and determined to lodge a complaint immediately but he did not want to leave the room for fear something else might happen. He spent the entire morning picking the papers up and carefully arranging them once more in their proper order.

These events were very disturbing. Then his eyes saw the corner of a sheet of paper protruding from behind a lamp. He pulled the paper out and stared at it curiously. The drawing on it seemed to be his own sketch and yet it did not.

He realized it was the one with which he had been dissatisfied. Something had been added, sketched in boldly, the drawing so altered that he scarcely recognized it. Someone had tampered with it! By now he was enraged. It had something to do with that foolish legend about this room, he supposed. The club staff must be trying to perpetuate it. Well, he would be out of here by noon, and as soon as he returned home, he would write the management a scathing letter of complaint on his company letterhead. Before he left, he would report to the concierge the disorder in which he had found his papers.

As Richard angrily snatched up the altered drawing and began to examine it, he began to feel a surge of intense excitement. Of course! Why hadn't he thought of this? The change in his drawing, indicated by the bold lines, was the key to making his idea work.

Only the most brilliant engineer could have devised this solution! For the first time in his life Richard Hayes believed in something outside of himself. He knew this concept was far beyond his own reach. Was it really the ghost of Samuel Spencer, perhaps in combination with a higher more heavenly power? He was filled with excitement and wonder.

. . . . . .

The Jekyll Island Club Hotel, 371 Riverview Drive, is recognized as a National Historic Landmark. J. P. Morgan and William Rockefeller dined by candlelight here, enjoying the fine view of the gardens and the Jekyll River available from the magnificent dining room. The modern-day cuisine is said to be superb, equaling that of the past. For information, phone 912-635-2600.